Archie AND THE ACCIDENTAL CHICKEN HEROES

Also by Anita Sachlikidis

Archie and the Accidental Chicken Heroes – The
Toxic Toads

~ Dragon Pets titles ~

Jasmine and the Hidden Treasures

Savannah and the Heart of Frost

Harley and the Stolen Splendour

Nari and the Lost Notes (coming soon)

Archie AND THE ACCIDENTAL CHICKEN HEROES

ANITA SACHLIKIDIS

To my own little family flock -
you're the best bunch of chicken
weirdos I could ask for.

**CLUCKY
FEATHERS**
— BOOKS —

Published by Clucky Feathers Books in 2024
Copyright © 2024 Anita Sachlikidis
Illustrations Copyright © 2024 Anita Sachlikidis
All rights reserved

ISBN-13: 978-0-9756132-2-1

We acknowledge the traditional custodians of the lands on which
we live and work, and where this book was written. We
acknowledge the cultural diversity of all Aboriginal and Torres
Strait Islander peoples and pay respect to Elders past, present
and future.

LOLA

ROSIE

OLIVE

COCO

THE SMALLS

Prologue

The lights on the Ferris wheel glittered brightly against the darkening sky. Over by the hot chip van the merry-go-round was a kaleidoscope of noise, colour and movement. Round and round and up and down shuffled an array of gaudy animals, accompanied by an assortment of excitable little riders all waggling arms and legs gleefully at bystander parents. But behind the brightly coloured elephants, dragons and horses, something more sinister was lurking. Hidden amongst the trees beyond the jagged shadows of the amusements, a frightening scenario was unfolding.

The boy stood with his feet planted, his face partly obscured by a faded feathery mask. He was facing a man dressed head to foot in dirty, faded navy blue work clothes and wearing a crazed look of determination. On the ground beside the man sat what looked like an old oven.

"You need to stop this! It's crazy!" the boy shouted. "I… I won't let you do it!"

The man gave a snort of laughter and turned to the oven-machine. He punched at a panel on its dented top and suddenly the front flashed bright with a brilliant glow of green, a flurry of numbers and letters appearing on a small screen.

"Seriously… you can't do this! You're going to hurt people. And… and…." stammered the boy.

"And what, boy? What? Those people out there? They'll get out of my way if they know what's good for them. And after tonight? No more fun fetes for the likes of you!"

The man gave another scornful laugh and turned his attention back to the oven-machine, waving his hand dismissively.

The boy felt his stomach clench. His fists balled up with angry tension. He felt desperate, hopeless even, as he watched the man in navy blue turn away from him as though he were no more than a pesky ant.

He took a deep breath and blew it out softly through his mouth. He felt helpless but he knew he had to try, he had to do SOMETHING. He glanced behind him into the thicket of trees beyond. Trying to calm the tremble in his voice, he spoke to the man again.

"I said, I won't let you do it. I'll stop you."

Not even bothering to turn and face him, the man replied, "Go home kid. You're on your own and there's nothing you can do to stop me. Whoever you are, it's better you just get out of here before it's too late."

The boy glanced behind him once more.

"I'm not on my own. And like I said, I WON'T let you do it."

He pursed his lips and whistled, then clucked his tongue twice. "Okay girls! It's time to teach this big bully a lesson. Let's go!"

From within the depths of the tree-lined darkness behind him there came... absolutely nothing.

He groaned inside and tried again.

"GIRLS! Come ON!"

The boy clucked his tongue three times more and spoke in a voice barely above a whisper, "Look. I KNOW you can do this. I'll... I'll double your feed tomorrow if you help me out here. PLEASE girls, come ON!"

For the briefest of moments, there was nothing more than the sound of a faint breeze swishing through the branches and the muted mutterings of the navy blue-clad man tinkering with his oven-machine.

And then, so slowly that it felt like time was standing still, here they came.

His girls. His CHICKENS.

Walking slowly but deliberately towards him and the crazy man.

With beady eyes and stiff wings held slightly aloft, the chickens moved forward to stand on either side of the small boy in his feathered mask.

The boy grinned and faced the man once more.

"I told you. I'm not alone. And now, my super chickens are here and together we will stop your evil plan!"

Chapter One: The Beginning

In the backyard of an ordinary suburban block a small boy dribbled a football around, the movements of his bare feet quick and deliberate. His light brown hair was tousled and there was a smudge on his forehead where he had pushed his sweaty hair off his face. The afternoon sun had just begun to dip low enough in the sky for the backyard to be draped in shade.

The boy, whose name was Archie, continued to kick the ball around, stopping it with his toe and moving his feet around as if he was a famous player in the World Cup. The round ball's slightly scuffed surface was patterned in pale blue and white - the colours of his Argentinian football idol Lionel Messi. As Archie dribbled the ball around he murmured a running commentary of the plays to himself.

"Messi passes to Archie. Archie side steps the defender... he shoots... he scores!! GOOOOAAAAALLL!!"

Archie jogged a victory lap around the yard, his arms outstretched and his face alight with imagined glory. As the cheering crowds dispersed and his imaginary football game reached its end he lowered his lanky frame to the ground. Archie sat cross-legged on the grass and watched the chickens pottering around the yard.

For the most part the chickens just ignored him. Every so often a bolder, more curious hen would wander closer, tilting their head to give him a good hard stare or to inspect a stray thread dangling from the hem of his shorts. Archie greeted this confidence with a light stroke of that chicken's smooth back feathers or a cheeky ruffle under the neck.

Ever since he'd been a small child, Archie could remember being around chickens. His first encounter had been at his grandma and grandad's place. They had a small property out of town that was much larger than Archie's house, but not quite large enough to be called a farm. His grandparents jokingly called it "The Ranch" and so that was what Archie grew to know it as. Alongside the smattering of fruit trees and the sprawling veggie patch, they kept a range of animals – chickens, a few noisy geese and an old dog named Reginald Fletcher.

Archie's best memories of his grandparents' property were when he was a little older and had started at school. Nearly every time school holidays came around, Archie's parents would pack up the car and head out to The Ranch. Sometimes they stayed just for the night or a few days and sometimes they stayed even longer. Archie had spent countless glorious hours exploring The Ranch, climbing trees and squatting in the dusty dry grass watching what the chickens were doing. Apart from their squat little rooster - who tended to glare suspiciously at Archie and issue vaguely threatening noises if he got too close to any of the hens – the chickens accepted Archie's presence. They even seemed to enjoy his company, especially if he arrived bearing gifts of squashed sandwich crusts and sticky watermelon rinds.

Archie's fondness of his grandparents' chickens had not gone unnoticed. It was his grandma who mentioned the idea one afternoon to his mum and dad. In her opinion, a boy with no siblings and two well-meaning but often busy parents might benefit from a little extra company around the home.

"Chickens make wonderful pets, you know - they're small, friendly and quite easy to look after," his grandma had argued. "And they lay eggs - well, at least some of the time, anyway!"

Archie's mum and dad had been reluctant at first but after some strong encouragement from his grandma (a chicken enthusiast at heart), they had agreed to get chickens when Archie was old enough to take responsibility for them.

"Well, you just let me know when you're ready," his grandma mused. "There's no shortage of chickens around these parts. I'll be sure to find you some right special chickens, just perfect for Archie." She winked at Archie, who was listening in with rapt attention.

And so it was that once Archie was old enough to dress himself and remember to brush his teeth twice a day, he found himself in possession of six new feathered friends. Six glorious young chickens of his very own. Sourced by his grandma as promised and transported to Archie's home in a large cardboard box safely nestled on the backseat. They were all hens - girl chickens - as a rooster was out of the question, given that Archie's home was in the middle of the suburbs. Archie was not especially disappointed about not having a noisy boy chicken, because although he admired the elegant plumage and vibrant colours typical of most roosters, he also remembered the sharp spurs and angry threats issued by his grandparents' rooster.

Instead he had his flock of six - a mix of brown, black and white seemingly normal hens. Naturally, after initially observing his chickens, Archie had given them all names. Over time the chickens relaxed into their new home, growing accustomed to their surroundings and to the presence of the small boy who looked after them. And in turn Archie was soon able to recognize each of his hens, noting that each had their own individual look and personality.

The boldest and most confident of his chickens was Lola, a medium-sized, fairly plain-looking brown chicken with a large red comb and perky tail. She carried herself with an air of plucky confidence that proclaimed her status as boss hen. Coco was light brown and slightly smaller than Lola, with a neat little face and sharp eyes that matched her bright, quick demeanour. His two largest chickens were Olive and Rosie, whose glistening feathers were a beautiful palette of green-black and red-brown respectively. Perhaps because of their larger size or perhaps because they just liked to, they spent much of their time sitting side by side, their heads bowed towards each other. Archie considered them to be like two old chicken grannies, settled down for a cup of tea and having a lovely old conversation.

The final two chickens in Archie's flock were a strange little pair - two white silkie chickens with feathers soft as cotton wool. Unlike his other chickens who had a red comb crowning the top of their heads, the silkies did not. Instead, they both had an oversized tuft of feathers sprouting from their heads like a fluffy pom-pom or a ridiculous tea cozy. They were much smaller than his other chickens, and their little legs were so short that their belly feathers brushed the grass as they wandered around the yard. Archie had named them Milk and Sugar, but he usually just called them the "Smalls" because they were, well, small.

Mostly the Smalls tottered around the yard so close to each other that they appeared to be joined together. They were so small that you could be forgiven for counting only five chickens instead of six.

A boy like Archie would have been besotted with his chickens even if they were the most ordinary of their kind.

But what his parents didn't know, nor anyone else for that matter, was that Archie's chickens were anything but ordinary. No. Every one of his girls had something about them that made them... different. Every one of Archie's chickens had a special talent. And Archie knew that no matter what anyone else thought, his chickens were NOT ordinary. They were EXTRAORDINARY.

Chapter Two: Meet The Chickens

He had discovered this secret about his chickens by accident. One swelteringly hot afternoon when Archie had been lying limply on the hammock staring at nothing, his mother had poked her head out the door.

"Archie," she said. "I just cleaned out the fridge. Here's some fruit and veggie scraps you can give to the chickens."

She held out a bowl overflowing with an assortment of soft, bruised-looking fruit and wilted leaves. On the top of the pile a wedge of watermelon balanced precariously, its pale red flesh dotted with black seeds.

Archie yawned lazily and swung his legs off the hammock, taking the bowl from her outstretched hand. "Okay Mum."

Opening the gate to the backyard, he walked through, holding the bowl with his arm extended and trying not to get any watermelon juice on his shirt front.

As Archie stepped onto the grass he felt something sticky dripping from the side of the bowl. He looked down and saw that a small, wet, pink spot had landed on his foot.

"Ugh. Gross."

The tiniest flutter of air brushed against his leg. All of a sudden he realized he was looking at a small, neat face closely inspecting the fresh spot on his foot.

"Coco! Where did you come from?" said Archie in surprise.

The little brown chicken had seemed to just appear next to his foot. Weird. Over the sickly sweet smell of the scraps he got a faint whiff of something burnt. Frowning slightly, Archie spotted some smoking black lines on the grass, barely visible amongst the lush green blades. He took a step forward to take a closer look. They looked like scorch marks. He raised his head again and looked back to where

Coco had just been standing beside him. Oddly, she was no longer there. She was now standing under the lemon tree on the opposite end of the backyard.

"Huh."

Archie gave his head a little shake. It must be the heat, he decided. Chickens can't move THAT fast.

He whistled and clucked his tongue to call the chickens. Finding a battered plastic tray on the grass he tipped the contents of the bowl into it. In an instant, there was that small, neat face again. Coco was right in front of him once more.

Archie was a little startled at her sudden appearance. He tried to shake off the niggling suspicion growing in his mind as the other chickens came running across the grass towards the food.

His biggest chicken, Rosie, was the first to arrive, her puffy backside swaying comically from her run across the grass. She hovered aggressively over Coco then gave her a sharp peck on the head.

"Rosie! Stop it!" scolded Archie. "You leave Coco alone."

He scooped Rosie up and tucked her under his arm. She gave a low chicken-growl of disapproval.

"Far out, you're heavy!"

Holding the empty bowl in one hand, he jiggled her into a better position on his hip.

The other chickens jostled around the food tray, fighting for space to peck at the soft wedge of watermelon. Lola was holding her wings out slightly away from her body, looking like she was trying to make herself solid and immovable. Still being harassed by the others, Coco moved swiftly out of range of their pecking beaks. Olive was issuing a steady stream of meaningful squawks, their intimidating message clear as she shoved the others bodily aside. The squawks grew higher in pitch, becoming more of a whistle than a squawk. Still growling, Rosie seemed to grow huge and even heavier in his arms. Archie found himself struggling to hold her.

It seemed to happen all in an instant.

In his arms Rosie was no longer of normal chicken proportions; instead, she seemed to have grown to the size of a small dog. The high-pitched whistling from Olive grew increasingly piercing, until it rose to a level that made Archie's ears tingle and then burn. They felt like they were about to burst. His hands flew to his ears. Rosie dropped to the ground with an almighty thud. The bowl he had been holding began to fall. Seemingly in slow-motion it looked certain to land directly on Lola, the chicken closest to Archie. And then Lola crouched, her wings curving out to form a shield above her, feathers glinting steely in the sunlight. The bowl hit the wing shield and shattered, pieces of white porcelain deflected away from Lola, away from Archie and scattered around the yard.

The whistling coming from Olive ceased. Archie looked around tentatively, lowering his hands from his ears. Rosie stood at Archie's feet, a huge and hulking mass of feathers reaching Archie's bottom in height. Coco was standing alone under the lemon tree. And the two smallest chickens, Milk and Sugar, stood off to the side looking, well, small.

Archie had no idea what had just happened.

He bolted out of the backyard and back into the house.

"Mum! Dad! Come here, quick!" yelled Archie. "You're not going to believe this!"

Dragging his parents into the backyard, Archie continued to shout in a loud and fast voice, sounding somewhere between a genius whose mouth couldn't keep up with the speed of his thoughts and a crazed scientist who had just made a breakthrough discovery.

"I was just giving them the scraps and Rosie was being mean to Coco so I picked her up and then Olive started making this AWFUL screeching noise and Rosie got HUGE and I couldn't hold her anymore and I dropped the bowl and it should have hit Lola, but she made this SHIELD and the bowl just bounced off her!"

Archie was breathing fast and his face was flushed with excitement. He gestured wildly over the backyard as the three of them stood, looking out.

Lola's wings hung neatly by her sides. The red and silver metallic sheen he had seen just a moment ago had vanished, smooth brown feathers in its place. Rosie was her normal size, sitting placidly on the grass next to Olive. The two of them were exchanging murmured clucks and soft chicken noises, with not a hint of ear-piercing whistling. Coco was walking around the yard at a relaxed pace, cropping at the grass. No sign of scorch marks remained. And the two smallest chickens were still, well, small.

Archie could not believe it. Had he imagined the whole thing?

His parents glanced at each other uneasily, looking both concerned and confused.

"Uh, Archie darling?" his mother said hesitantly. "You did just give all those old scraps to the chickens, didn't you? You didn't… eat any yourself? Or fall out of the hammock and bump your head?"

"What? No!" spluttered Archie. "Why would I - I didn't - I'm not making it up!"

His parents stared at the chickens, who were at that moment behaving like normal, ordinary and entirely unremarkable chickens.

They both smiled gently at him and turned to go back to the house. His dad ruffled him on the head. "Good to see you haven't lost your imagination, buddy."

"But they really were… they really did…"

Archie's voice trailed off. Had he just imagined the whole thing?

After his parents had both left he lingered, staring at the chickens with his arms hanging loosely by his sides, before dropping to a cross-legged position on the ground.

He narrowed his eyes and focused his gaze on the hens more closely. Coco lifted her head and very quickly glanced around, looking shifty.

Seeming to notice Archie's watchful gaze she just as quickly resumed cropping the grass, head down and eyes averted in an attempt to avoid suspicion. Olive and Rosie continued to murmur soft chicken noises, their heads tilted towards each other. They kept pausing and throwing sideways glances in his direction.

A soft padding of footsteps drew his attention away from the two sitting chickens. Lola was standing directly in front of him and staring straight on, her beady eyes narrowed as she appraised him. It was rather unnerving having a chicken stare at you in this manner, instead of tilting its head to the side. Archie had a strong suspicion that Lola was weighing him up in some way. He cupped his hands to her sides and picked her up, searching her unblinking eyes for answers.

"What just happened? Was it all in my head?"

Lola continued to stare at him in silence. Archie felt even more confused than before. He placed Lola down on the ground and slowly walked back to the house, six pairs of watchful eyes trained on him the entire way.

Chapter Three: School Day

The next day was a school day and Archie headed in through the school gates with his bag slung over his shoulder. He was somewhat relieved to be back on familiar grounds. Back to a place where his days followed a predictable routine that he knew and understood. His encounter with the chickens had left him feeling all sorts of things that he couldn't get his head around. At the time he had been so SURE, so certain that it had ACTUALLY happened… but doubt had crept into his mind and clouded his memory. Had the bright sunlight caused Lola's feathers to take on the look and sheen of steel blades? Maybe he'd been lying on the hammock too long, deadening his arm so that Rosie felt unnaturally heavy? Perhaps his senses had been dulled by the stifling heat, making him feel like he was moving through thick clay and not seeing things as they really were.

But it really did happen, the small voice in his mind whispered. *You didn't imagine it. It wasn't just a dream.*

Archie decided to try and put the whole incident aside, at least until he had more time to properly observe his chickens. He deposited his school bag on the rack next to a familiar black and green backpack and headed off in search of his best friend.

It wasn't long before he spotted the shaggy blonde head of his friend Josh amongst the throng of students. Josh was in the undercover walkway behind their classroom, holding a stretchy man figurine and heading towards the shady playground area. They fell into step chatting easily as they went.

"Cool stretchy man!" said Archie.

"Yeah, I got it at Timezone! My cousin Ben had a birthday party yesterday and that's where it was," said Josh with a broad, happy grin on his face.

"Aww, I love Timezone, that place is AWESOME. Did you go on the dodgem cars?"

"Nah. We had these passes that you swiped to play the games and the dodgem cars weren't included," replied Josh. "But you got to choose a prize from the shop at the end using points you won from the games. I could have gotten another bouncy ball or a mini skateboard, but they only had red balls left and I already have a red one, so I decided on this instead."

Several of Archie's classmates were already at the playground. They crowded around Josh to get a look at his new stretchy man.

First, they tried to get the stretchy man to reach between the gaps of the monkey bars. That didn't last long. It was too hard to hold onto both the climbing frame AND the little man.

"Hey Josh, let's use him as a slingshot!" said Ryan, a short, heavily freckled boy who often played with Archie and Josh even though he wasn't in their class.

Archie dug two sticks into the dirt about a hand's width apart. Ryan and Josh pinned the stretchy man's little arms and legs to the sticks with their fingers, before pulling his body back to send a pebble flying. Other kids used sand, dirt and leaves to build up tiny forts for the stretchy man slingshot to aim at. The targets and projectiles grew more and more ruthless and soon the game had turned into all-out war. Sticks and handfuls of pebbles scooped into leaf-cups were strewn all over the playground and the adjacent walkway. Archie was just about to toss a scrunched-up leaf grenade when the sudden appearance of a pair of heavy black boots on the footpath stole his attention. Looming over him was Mr Franksman, the school groundskeeper.

Mr Franksman was very tall, with a thin, angular face and dark eyes that clouded his face like clouds full of the promise of rain. His dark, almost black hair was cut short all over and was usually pressed under a wide-brimmed hat.

The groundskeeper's uniform of black boots,

navy blue pants and button-down shirt was supplemented with a toolbelt fastened tightly around his waist. Archie could see tools and pencils sticking out of the toolbelt, as well as various objects clipped onto his belt loops.

With a scowl on his face, Mr Franksman's gaze swept over the group of boys, his eyes narrowing as he took in the scattered debris and piles of dirt, fallout from the stretchy man slingshot war.

The boisterous game fell instantly silent. Mr Franksman had that effect on the students. He was an intimidating figure, stomping around the school looking brooding and ominous.

"You boys need to keep your mess off the path, do you hear?" he said in a low, cold voice.

"Sorry Mr Franksman!" squeaked Archie, trying to appear cool and nonplussed but betrayed by his high-pitched voice. Ryan hurriedly tried to gather up a pile of sticks and leaves closest to him, but as he bent over a loud fart escaped from his bottom.

He flushed pink in the face and moved even faster in his efforts to clean up. The boys around him

25

stifled their sniggers, fearful of laughing openly in front of the groundskeeper, but at least the fart had helped to ease the tension.

With a final glare at Archie, Mr Franksman started up the super high-powered leaf blower, aimed it at the scattered debris and blasted the offending lot off the path and back into the playground.

The boys all scattered, Josh quickly scooping up his stretchy man before sprinting off after Archie.

When they had put a safe distance between themselves and the disgruntled groundskeeper, Josh let out a low whistle.

"He is one cranky man, Mr Franksman."

"Yeah, he is SERIOUSLY cranky, like ALL the time," said Archie.

"You get like ONE LEAF on the path and he stomps over and tells you off!"

"Yeah! It's like he's got some kind of fun radar that detects when there's too much fun stuff going on and then he's all over it in a second."

"Totally!" laughed Josh. "Maybe when he's holed up in his shed he's working on evil plans."

"Haha, sounds about right to me!"

They jokingly shared wild theories, dissolving into fits of laughter as their evil groundskeeper plots grew more and more ridiculous.

"Swapping all the school erasers for stinky old cheese."

"Getting the tuckshop to only sell salad sandwiches made with the crusts from the end of the bread loaf."

"Putting booger slime on the water bubbler handles."

"Swapping the school photos for pictures of everyone as babies wearing nothing but stinky nappies."

"Filling the soap dispensers with super glue."

"Forcefield around the football goals so nobody can score."

"Sinkholes in the oval."

"Reversing the air conditioners so they blow hot air in summer and cold in winter."

"Putting fart bombs into the air vents to stink out all the classrooms."

27

The first bell signalling the start of the school day rang out. Still giggling, Archie and Josh stowed their hats in their bags and headed into the classroom.

At the playground, Mr Franksman took one final look around, satisfied that order had been restored to the walkways once more. He retreated to his work shed, giving no indication of anything that would support the boys' jokes about evil plots and sinister plans.

The rest of the school day continued with little incident to speak of. It passed in a blur of books opening, books being packed away, lunchboxes opening and their contents being consumed or discarded, depending on the appeal of the provisions within.

Finally, just before the sounding of the bell signalling the end of the school day, their teacher, Miss Mitchum, handed out a sheet to each of the students. Across the top of the sheet the headline "School Fete" was emblazoned in large, bold letters.

"It's an information leaflet about the upcoming school Fete," said Miss Mitchum. "Please pass it on to your parents."

A ripple of excitement swept through the class. The school Fete was the most exciting night of the term. The most exciting night of the whole year, if you didn't count the Halloween Disco. As the bell rang and the kids streamed out of the classroom, discussion centred around the Fete and the glorious rides, games and food to be had. Those who had already experienced the Fete in previous years compared stories of eating too much fairy floss and feats of glory at the Dunk a Teacher stand. Those who had never been to the Fete listened on with envy, clutching the information leaflet with their eyes roving hungrily over its list of promised delights.

As the school emptied and cars dispersed towards their various destinations, a lone figure walked along the path near the main school gate. They scooped up a stray piece of paper, their eyes drifting over the words "School Fete" emblazoned across its top. For a moment they stood still, as if hypnotized.

Then they turned abruptly and strode off, the echo of heavy boots on pavement fading as they disappeared from sight.

Chapter Four: Archie's Discovery

After another ordinary day at school, the end-of-day bell rang out. Today however, instead of heading to the gates where the parents and cars gathered, Archie headed towards the oval for football practice. His parents had signed him up for a term of special training sessions that were held every Tuesday afternoon.

About twenty students milled around under the trees at the edge of the school oval. Archie flopped down on the ground. He pulled off his school shoes and wriggled his feet into his football boots. One of the coaches, Jesse, stood off to the side with his foot resting on a football. He flicked the ball up with the toe of his boot and began juggling it with his right foot.

Archie finished tying up his left boot. The coach was now bouncing the ball on his knee, alternating from left to right.

Archie quickly tied up his right boot laces. Coach Jesse bounced the ball a final time and trapped the ball with his foot on the ground, throwing Archie a grin.

"How's it going Archie?" he said.

"Pretty good, Coach Jesse," said Archie. "That was so cool!"

Coach Jesse grinned at him again before heading over to join the head coach, ready to start the session.

"Okay guys and girls. Gather round and listen up," said the head coach, as Archie and the rest of the group stood and clustered around him and Coach Jesse.

"Today we're going to start with some training drills, working on your dribbling and passing and then defensive skills. And if we have time at the end of our session, we'll have a quick game of Clean the Room to finish up. Sound good?"

There was a chorus of agreement from the group. Clean the Room was a popular game that everyone liked and they were all keen to get started. They moved out onto the oval where a series of bright orange markers were already laid out in formation.

The afternoon training session moved along more or less as it usually did. Most of the kids tried hard and did their best to follow what the coaches said. Some of the drills were a bit tricky to master. A couple of kids struggled and got frustrated with themselves. Coach Jesse drifted among the group, offering words of encouragement and help where needed. They moved through the training drills steadily, stopping only for drink breaks and further instruction from the head coach.

Finally, as the session was drawing to the end, the markers were collected and the group gathered together in a little huddle. This time it was Coach Jesse who spoke to them.

"Okay folks! Most of you are already familiar with the rules of Clean the Room, but I'll give you a quick run-through just to make sure everyone's clear. We're playing on that small pitch, split into two halves." As he said this Jesse gestured with his arm towards the smaller playing area on the oval used by the junior school students.

"You guys start with all the balls on your half of the field. That's your 'Room'. Us coaches will be on the other half. Your goal is to clean your 'Room' of any balls by kicking them into our half of the field. We'll be doing our best to kick the balls back into your room. Everyone with me so far?"

There was a flurry of nodding and "Yes Coach Jesse'"s.

"Great! Alright. A quick game's a good game! And just to motivate you a bit more, if there are any balls in your room when the whistle blows, that's how many laps you'll be doing at the start of next week's session!" finished Coach Jesse, grinning.

"Oh, what!?"

"No fair!"

"We'll show you!"

The group banter at this last declaration from Coach Jesse continued as they all ran out onto their half, where about ten balls were already scattered around. Coach Jesse's laughing reply floated back to them, "Don't want laps? Well work hard and keep those balls out of your Room!"

The two coaches positioned themselves in the other half of the small pitch. The head coach blew his whistle and the game of Clean the Room got underway in a mad rush of balls flying, legs pumping and gleeful laughter on both sides.

*　　　*　　　*

Archie stood bent over at the waist, his chest heaving as he drew in huge, gasping breaths. His legs burned with tiredness and his face ached from laughing. He and the others had had so much fun! It felt so good, running and kicking and running and kicking. He'd even managed to boot one glorious shot clear over both coaches. Even now he couldn't help grinning, recalling how sweet it had felt when his boot connected just right, how he had paused to watch the ball soaring in a splendid arc through the air.

In the end, just two balls had not been cleared from the Room. Most of the others littered the coaches' half, but a couple of balls had been kicked clear of both fields to the cluster of trees at the far edge of the school oval.

Coach Jesse walked up to him, a ball tucked under one arm.

"Nice work today Archie! Saw your massive kick back there. Channelling Messi eh?" he said.

Archie just grinned and looked down at his boots, too chuffed with the compliment to say anything.

"Now run along and collect those couple of balls out there before warm-down," he laughed, ruffling Archie's hair with his free hand.

Still grinning, Archie sprinted off towards the trees. He picked up the first ball and jogged over to where the second one had come to rest after his glorious kick. He tucked the second ball under an arm and was about to turn and race back when he heard a noise. Something that did not fit with the gentle rustlings of plants and scurrying movements of birds and other small creatures in the undergrowth. No, this was more of a whirring, mechanical sort of noise. Archie stood still, listening. Then he heard a clang of metal and the muffled mutterings of a voice. A man's voice.

"What the..?" he half-whispered to himself. He glanced quickly back towards the school. The rest of the group were collecting the on-field balls and a few were already heading back to where the coaches stood at the edge of the oval.

For a brief moment Archie considered ignoring the odd sounds. He could just pretend that he had heard nothing, that he had imagined it. He could turn around and head back, re-join his teammates.

But instead, he turned back to face the trees and the strange noises. He swallowed nervously, then very quietly and carefully began to move forward. Towards the sound of the man's voice, towards the muttering and whirring that grew louder with each step he took. Gripping the balls more tightly, he ducked under a low, leafy branch. As he straightened up he spotted a tall, lanky figure in the shadows, standing next to whatever it was that was making the strange noises.

A figure clad in navy blue that Archie knew all too well.

Archie stifled a gasp of shock and surprise. He crept forward, keeping himself hidden behind the trees. When he had moved as close as he dared, he crouched down low behind a small shrub and tried to remember how to breathe normally. He peered through the scratchy leaves, his gaze travelling over a small open space within the trees.

In the middle of the clearing stood Mr Franksman the groundskeeper.

Archie could not think of a single good reason for Mr Franksman to be out here, at this time of day, all alone in the middle of the forest.

The man was hunched over what looked like an old oven.

Except it also DIDN'T look like an oven.

There was an extra panel on the top that gave off an eerie glow in the dim light. Numbers and symbols flashed on a small screen as the groundskeeper alternated between punching buttons on the top panel and fiddling with an elaborate tangle of wires connecting through to the back of the machine.

The machine was emitting a low humming sound and from within its main body a glowing light pulsed almost as if it were alive.

From behind his trusty shrub, Archie watched as Mr Franksman tightened something with a screwdriver. Then he stepped back and stared at the machine, a look of triumph on his face. Replacing the screwdriver in his toolbelt and wiping his hands on his pants, Mr Franksman bent over the machine and carefully punched a series of buttons. There was a slight pause before Mr Franksman's hand travelled across the panel to hover over a large, red button.

Archie held his breath.

"Here goes nothing..." muttered the groundskeeper and with a sweaty, trembling finger he pressed the red button.

The machine whirred into life. It sounded like something was spinning, faster and faster. The body of the machine glowed brighter and brighter, a blinding whirl of light emanating from within. Archie saw Mr Franksman take several tentative steps backwards.

All of a sudden the whirring reached a crescendo and with a blinding flash a whirling portal appeared. The air around the portal seemed to crackle with energy, bright sparks flashing around the edges of the swirling depths.

Mr Franksman gave a harsh bark of triumph and raised his hands in the air.

Archie watched in mute horror, frozen with fear.
RRRRARRRGGGGGHHAAAKKKK!!!

Suddenly, from within the portal there came a deep and terrifying roar. It was a shrieking cry that threatened terrible and immediate danger. Like a huge, wild and angry creature was about to burst from the portal. It sounded very much like a monster... like a dinosaur!

RRRRARRRRRGGGGGHHHHHEEEKKKK!!!

Another roar bellowed out of the depths of the machine. It sounded closer this time and more threatening.

The groundskeeper was standing on the tips of his toes, his hands now clutching his face which was lit up with equal parts delight and terror.

Still crouching in his leafy hiding place, Archie could barely breathe. His whole body was paralyzed with fear. In some distant part of his brain, he knew he needed to move, to get as far away from whatever was making that hair-raising sound. He willed his legs to take action but they no longer seemed to be under his control.

But before Archie could summon any life back into his limbs, the noises from the machine ceased. A silence fell across the little clearing as heavy as a wool blanket. The whirling portal had disappeared and the glowing lights on the machine were dark, the top panel now blank and silent.

The man in navy blue cursed. His hands fell away from his face and he kicked at the leaves on the ground in frustration.

Archie blew out a breath he hadn't realized he had been holding. He was trembling all over, but at least his legs seemed to be working again. His arms were still locked around the balls he had retrieved.

With a last swift glance at the groundskeeper and his malfunctioning machine, he turned and began creeping out of the forest.

When he reached the edge of the trees he did not look back. He sprinted as fast as he could back across

41

the oval, the two balls clutched tightly to his hammering chest. He quickly joined the rest of his teammates sprawled on the grass, his mind churning with what he had just witnessed.

Chapter Five: Food For Thought

Lying on his bed later that afternoon, Archie's head was reeling. His mind was a whirl of questions. What had Mr Franksman been doing? Had he really seen and heard what he thought he had? Or was it just a trick of his mind, a product of his overactive imagination and being hot and tired after a long day of school and football?

Archie sighed and rolled off his bed. It was no use just lying here, his mind full of questions he could not answer. What he really wanted was to DO something about it. He was certain the bad-tempered groundskeeper was plotting something. Why else would he be lurking about in the trees? He knew he needed to keep an eye on him, find out what he planned to do. But how?

He picked up a book lying on the floor and absently rifled through its pages. His eye was drawn to an image of a strong, crouching figure wielding a shield. On the next page several more characters grouped around the shield-wielding hero, poised in battle pose with determination written on their faces. They looked fierce, ready for anything. A team of heroes banded together against the enemy!

If only I wasn't on my own, thought Archie. *If I just had a team to help me, or…*

Suddenly Archie sat up straight. Maybe… maybe he DID have a team!

Archie tossed the book onto his bed and dashed out to the backyard.

He called out to the chickens.

"Girls! Here girls!"

Archie walked across the grass, placing his feet carefully to avoid stepping in chicken poo. He clucked his tongue several times and before he had gone too far the flock came trotting out to meet him.

To Archie's disappointment, not one of the chickens was doing anything other than being plain old ordinary chickens. The four largest chickens - Rosie, Olive, Lola and Coco – milled around at his feet, peering up at Archie curiously. The Smalls had barely moved, huddled off to the side looking slightly bewildered, their silly puff of head feathers obscuring all but the tips of their beaks.

Archie thought back to the hot afternoon when he had first discovered his chickens' secret. He willed himself to recall every detail, searching his memories for a clue, for some vital key to unlocking his chickens' abilities. He remembered how Coco had appeared so suddenly at his feet. How he had struggled to support the dead weight of Rosie under one arm. And then that unbearable whistle, an intense high-pitched NOISE that had spilled out of Olive and nearly brought him to his knees. The steely glint of Lola's wing-shield, the immense bulk of giant Rosie thudding onto the ground. The empty scrap bowl slipping from his fingers, hitting the wing-shield and shattering into pieces. Standing and staring in disbelief at the remains of the watermelon wedge, its soft flesh pockmarked with beak-shaped gashes.

Food, he thought. *Food could be the key.*

Archie glanced down at the chickens, before turning and heading towards the small garden shed tucked in one corner of the yard. He unlatched the door and it swung open with a rusty whine. Removing the lid from a large metal bin, Archie lifted out a scoop of grain in a chipped green enamel mug.

The chickens had followed him expectantly, their eyes trailing his movements greedily. He held the mug aloft, waving it slowly from side to side. Six chicken heads traced an arc that mirrored the mug's path.

He moved the mug up and down. The chicken heads obediently nodded up and down.

Archie whirled the mug in front of him, turning a full circle. The chickens swivelled their heads dumbly. Archie watched the six chicken heads rotating slowly, matching pace with the mug held in his swinging arm.

He swung his arm faster. The heads swivelled faster.

Come on, Archie willed. *Do something different. Something special.*

He tried swinging even faster. The mug was now just a green blur fixed to the end of his arm. By this point he was starting to make himself dizzy.

The chickens did not try to speed up. One by one they stopped moving their heads. Lola and Coco looked at Archie with a somewhat disappointed expression. Rosie growled and glared at him grumpily. The others just looked dazed and confused.

Archie stopped swinging the mug, feeling deflated. He tried to stem his growing disappointment by imagining the situation through someone else's eyes. An onlooker would probably find the whole thing quite amusing. It was funny really - just a silly little prank, using food to trick the chickens into moving their heads like laughing clowns at a sideshow alley. Still, it was hard for Archie to find it funny, not when he was so determined for his chickens to act, well, NOT like chickens.

He retrieved the plastic food tray and emptied the contents of the mug into it. A little of the grain spilled onto the grass. As the chickens converged on the tray, Archie stepped back and waited for something to happen.

Any moment now, he thought. *No wait – I need to pick up Rosie first.*

He bent to grab Rosie but she scooted backwards and out of reach. The others shuffled over and continued pecking at the grain.

Archie groaned in frustration.

He picked up the tray and sprinted as fast as he could to the other end of the yard, coming to an abrupt stop under the lemon tree.

He had hoped that Coco would have already made her way over to him, leaving scorched grass in her wake. Or that the departure of the food tray would send Olive into a whistling frenzy. Instead, both Coco and Olive remained near the other chickens, scratching around for spilled grain where Archie had first placed the tray.

In desperation, Archie decided to make one last ditch effort. He ran yelling into the midst of the flock. Then he threw the plastic tray high into the air. A shower of grain rained down, landing on the backs of the chickens like tiny speckled hailstones. The tray flipped in the air, then plummeted towards Lola who deftly stepped out of the way at the very last second.

Archie stood watching them, crestfallen. This had not gone at all as he had hoped.

There had not been even one single sign of anything extraordinary. His chickens had not displayed any special talents or given any indication that they were anything other than normal, regular chickens.

He ran a hand through his hair, dislodging a few stray grains onto the grass. The chickens murmured happy, contented clucks as they moved around, hunting for hidden treasures in the green blades.

With a last forlorn look at the chickens, who continued to behave like ordinary chickens, Archie turned and went back inside the house feeling more uncertain than ever.

Chapter Six: Chicken Convention

As the other chickens continued combing over the backyard lawn, Lola lifted her head and watched the small departing figure. When he had stepped into the house and shut the door behind him, she turned to the rest of the flock.

"Right! Come on you lot - we're having a chicken meeting under the lemon tree. Let's go!"

She marched off briskly towards the lemon tree, with the others following behind shortly after.

"Alright girls, huddle up," said Lola. "Olive, Coco, Rosie, that's good. Yes, nice and close so we can all hear. Now. We need to talk about our Chicken-Boy. Hang on. Where are the Smalls? Smalls??"

"We're right here," said two small voices in unison. It sounded like it was coming from Rosie's fluffy bottom. Then a puffy white head, closely followed by a second, popped up between Rosie and Olive.

"Oh! Sorry! Didn't see you there!" said Lola. "Sorry. It's just that you're so, well, small."

The Smalls just stared at Lola. Or at least, they might have been staring at Lola. It really was impossible to tell with their giant feather pom-poms.

"Ok. Well. Never mind, let's carry on then…" Lola continued. "Now. As you might have noticed, it seems that Chicken-Boy has learned of our special talents. And going by his most recent fumbling attempts, he wants us to show him them again. The question is – what do we do about it now?"

Lola turned her bright eyes to each of the chickens in turn. Coco was staring at the ground, closely inspecting a piece of grass near one foot. Rosie gave a big grumpy huff and settled herself down, fluffing her feathers out so she resembled a round, puffy galleon in full sail.

Lola tried again. "Okay then. Do we like Chicken-Boy? Can we trust him?"

52

Olive blinked at Lola. "Chicken-Boy brings us food. I like food," said Olive. "I think we should… we should… food! FLYING FOOD!!"

At these last words, Olive had bolted off in pursuit of a dragonfly hovering low over the grass. Her neck darted left and then right as the dragonfly, sensing danger, began flitting away. Olive hopped as high as she could with her neck comically outstretched, but the

dragonfly had flown up into the air and just out of reach.

"Olive!" snapped Lola. "Focus!"

"Sorry! Sorry!" squawked Olive. Her eyes were bulging and she looked slightly deranged. "Right. Chicken-Boy is a nice boy. If he were smaller, I would let him share my perch. Yes. I think Chicken-Boy would be a fine perch-mate. If he were not so big. And if he continues to bring food. I do like food."

"But even if he were smaller, he has the most AWFUL feathers!" said Rosie scornfully. "His feathers are so small and puny and are always in such a mess. He must not spend any time taking care of his feathers at all! No, I would not want to share a perch with him. Imagine having those awful feathers right next to my fine plumage! Disgusting!"

"Feathers do not matter so much," said Olive. "Not as long as you have food."

"What good is food if you have no feathers? The best chickens always have beautiful feathers," retorted Rosie.

"Food is best!" squawked Olive, her voice rising in pitch.

"No, feathers are best!"

"Food!"

"FEATHERS!"

"FOOD!!"

By this stage Rosie had risen to her feet, her feathers puffed out and bristling with growing fury. Olive's words had emerged as more of a whistle, though not yet at ear-piercing shrillness.

"GIRLS!" squawked Lola. "Chicken-Boy is NOT going to share our coop! Food and feathers are BOTH important! This is NOT HELPFUL!"

She glared at Rosie and Olive, who looked slightly sheepish. They settled themselves into a less confrontational stance, though Rosie continued to grumpily mutter something under her breath about feathers.

"Where were we?" said Lola. "Oh yes. What do we think of Chicken-Boy? Coco? Any thoughts?"

At the sound of her name Coco's head shot up and she gave a tiny squawk of surprise. She was quite a jittery chicken.

"What? Oh right, ok, yes Chicken-Boy, Chicken-Boy...," blurted Coco.

She paused to preen nervously at a spot on her neck before continuing, her words spewing out all in a rush.

"Well, I personally think Chicken-Boy is a very nice boy yes very nice indeed though you have a good point Rosie about his feathers being quite awful and ragged and lacking in care and not nearly as beautiful as yours of course and as Olive said he does give us food at least every day and sometimes more than once a day and food is a very good thing too we all like food especially the very nice food that Chicken-Boy brings."

This time it was Lola who stood blinking as Coco continued her verbal deluge.

"As well as the bringing of food I think Chicken-Boy is a nice boy very nice as I said before though he does seem to be a bit stupid sometimes and perhaps does not have a very large brain even though he does have a very large head under those awful puny feathers and I think that maybe if he did not have a tiny brain then he would perhaps not do things that are a tiny bit stupid and we would not think of him as a very nice tiny-brained Chicken-Boy with ugly feathers."

Lola regarded Coco for a moment. Then she began to pace back and forward under the lemon tree, apparently deep in thought.

"So," said Lola. "So… we agree that Chicken-Boy is a nice boy -"

Both Rosie and Olive opened their beaks to interrupt but Lola quickly cut them off.

"- a nice boy who – food, feathers and tiny brain aside – seems to have good intentions," she continued. "It is clear that he wants to see what we can do and what our powers are."

"Why would he be interested in our powers?" said Coco.

"Maybe he thinks we can help him grow some decent feathers and look more respectable," suggested Rosie.

Lola gave her a hard stare. Rosie mumbled something under her breath but kept her head down.

From behind Rosie came a small noise, like a muffled cough.

All the chickens turned towards the noise. Behind Rosie stood the Smalls, the pair of them clumped together like squashed marshmallows.

"Maybe he just..." said Milk.

"...needs our help," finished Sugar.

They stood silently digesting this. It was another few moments before anyone spoke again.

"Ok. Right!" said Lola. "Here's what I think. If the Smalls are correct and Chicken-Boy does need our help... well. If Chicken-Boy can just stop being so stupid and simply ASK us for help, I think we should trust him and go to his aid."

She puffed out her chest, stood a little straighter.

"Chicken-Boy is our friend and we will use our powers to help him!"

There was a chorus of enthusiastic clucking. Lola made her way round the little group high-fiving with her wing. She got past Rosie and Coco, but the Smalls couldn't see what she was doing and left her wing hanging in mid-air. And then Olive spotted a lizard creeping along the rocks by the fence and dashed towards it, crashing into Lola and bowling over the Smalls in the process.

Chapter Seven: Commands And Consistency

Archie had tried to put his unsuccessful super-chicken discovery attempt behind him. He went to school and football training as usual, doing everything he could to put the whole business of chicken powers at the back of his mind. This turned out to be surprisingly easy to do at school. He was so busy playing and hanging out with his friends that it was easy to be distracted.

However, staying distracted was proving difficult when Archie was at home. Each time Archie ventured into the backyard to kick his ball around, surrounded by his girls clucking and ambling around, he was reminded of that hot afternoon. Coco's lightning-fast movements. Olive's whistle piercing the air. Rosie's giant hulking frame thudding on the ground. The sheen of Lola's steely wing-shield.

This afternoon, Archie was outside in the backyard. He'd just fed the chickens and was standing around watching them eat, holding the old green mug he'd used to scoop the feed.

As usual, the chickens were squabbling for the best position around the food tray. A murmur of warning sounds issued from the bigger hens, overlaid with a steady rumble of growling from Rosie.

Archie thought of this as a kind of feeding time dance, each of the chickens shuffling around in a predictable rhythm. Olive would step to the side and Lola and Rosie would follow, shuffling sideways in a clumsy chicken waltz.

Archie giggled to himself as he imagined the chickens stepping up their dance routine, puffing out their chests and flicking their wing feathers out in a flourish. He pictured Rosie's puffy backside twirling around like a ballroom gown and Coco and Lola locking wing-tips in a quick-stepping chicken jive.

As he stood watching the chickens engaged in their dance routine, his neighbour Tom emerged from the house next door. Tom frequently spent time in his yard watering or weeding the garden and more often than not he would have a chat with Archie through the fence. He headed towards the vegie patch dragging a snaking garden hose behind him.

"Hey Archie. How's it going?" called Tom.

"Alright," replied Archie.

"Dinner time for the chickens hey? Must be their favourite time of day." Tom squeezed the trigger nozzle and began hosing the bean plants, their leafy tendrils winding up and over a wire trellis.

Archie didn't say anything. He watched as Tom gave the hose a twirl to unravel a kink.

Tom's little dog, Nick Furry, came trotting down the yard towards them. Nick was a smart little French bulldog with a large personality and even larger ears. The combined effect of his huge ears and his wrinkled little face made him look both alert and slightly confused, like he'd just forgotten the punchline to a really good joke. As he came closer to the fence Lola gave a sharp squawk of alarm, causing the chickens to raise their heads towards the apparent threat. Nick swivelled his huge batlike ears towards the sound and barked.

"Nick. Quiet!" called Tom. The little dog gave a final triumphant bark, as if having the last word in an argument, before falling silent and trotting over to his master with his tail wagging.

"Nick. Sit!"

Obediently, the little dog dropped his bottom to the grass. The chickens gave the dog a hard stare before returning their attention to the food.

Archie had a sudden thought. "Tom..." he started. "How did you get Nick Furry to do what you say? Did you train him?"

"Who, this little troublemaker? Yeah, I suppose he does listen to me most of the time," said Tom, reaching down and giving Nick a playful rub behind the ears. "I took him to obedience training classes at first. That's where he learned all of his basic commands. But I still have to work with him. Training any animal is something you have to keep doing all the time. You have to be consistent with animals, see, otherwise they just get confused and ignore you."

Archie considered this.

"So... how did you get him to start listening to you?"

"That's an easy one. He loves his doggie treats, Nick does, so I made sure I had a pocketful of his favourites before I started any training session. That way, when he followed a command correctly, I had a reward to give to him straightaway. Plus a good old pat too, of course!"

Nick Furry grinned a toothy dog grin up at Tom, as if to say, "Couldn't have put it better myself!"

Tom continued, "So once you've got the key to what motivates them, or how to reward them, you need to focus on how you communicate. Talk in a language they understand, so to speak. Simple commands work best. Oh, and you have to listen to what they're telling you. Animals are very good at letting you know what they're thinking. It's just that most people don't bother to pay enough attention."

Archie digested all this information. Tom had now moved on to watering the pumpkin patch. He used his foot to nudge aside the large green leaves, checking the progress of the growing pumpkins tucked amongst the sprawling vine like hidden gems.

"Don't tell me your parents are thinking of getting a dog?" asked Tom.

Archie shook his head. "Nah. Mum and Dad say they're too busy to have a dog. Plus, a dog might eat my chickens."

Tom grinned. "Fair enough. So, you're thinking of training your chickens then?"

Archie looked a little sheepish. That was EXACTLY what he had been thinking.

"Maybe," he admitted. "Though, I don't know if you really can train chickens. They're supposed to be, well, kind of stupid."

Tom threw his head back and laughed. Archie forced himself to laugh too, throwing a guilty glance at the chickens. Lola and Olive were staring at him, their narrowed eyes glaring as if they'd understood exactly what he'd just said and found it extremely insulting.

"Well, if anyone was going to be able to train chickens, it'd be you Archie! I'm sure you'll figure it out."

Tom gave the garden a final spray and released the trigger nozzle.

"Good luck!" he said as he headed off, looping the hose as he went.

Archie watched as Tom turned off the tap and hung the looped hose over a hook.

He folded his legs and sat down cross-legged on the grass, the enamel feed mug circled in his hands. There was still a little grain in the bottom that he'd held back, planning on hand feeding it to one of his girls later on.

The chickens were milling around on the grass, having finished the food that Archie had delivered earlier. Nick Furry was busily sniffing around Tom's yard, most likely enjoying the smells of the freshly wet garden. He lifted his wrinkled face and looked quizzically at Archie before continuing his nose-first exploration of the pumpkin patch.

Chapter Eight: Chicken Breakthrough

Archie pondered the conversation he'd just had with Tom. He was still determined to unlock the secret to the chicken's powers and after some reflection, he considered that maybe he'd been going about it the wrong way. Of course the chickens wouldn't be persuaded by ordinary chicken food. After all, they ate it every day, so why would they deem it a worthy reward for extraordinary skills? Now that he thought about it, trying to spook or trick the chickens into exceptional behaviour did seem a bit silly, maybe even a little insulting. No. He needed to think of something clearer, more consistent.

Archie got up and went back into the house. He returned shortly after wearing a cap and bearing a notepad and pencil, as well as the green mug which he had filled with grated pizza cheese from a bag in the fridge. He shook a pile of cheese into his hand and stuffed it into one pocket, then did the same for his other pocket. Taking the cap off his head, he placed the old enamel mug on the grass and covered it with the cap so as to hide the remaining cheese from the chickens.

Resettling himself into a cross-legged position, he drew out the notepad and opened it to a blank page. Archie wrote Super Chickens at the top of the page and underlined it twice. He paused to think for a minute, then began writing underneath the heading.

Pocket rewards - cheese, grapes, sandwich crusts

Archie could think of plenty of other things his chickens loved as treats, but it was a bit hard to imagine squeezing old bananas and sticky watermelon into his pockets. Gross. And he knew his mum and dad would be totally disgusted if they turned out his pants pockets and found bits of canned fish crusted onto the insides.

He scrawled another heading - Commands - and below that listed the names of each of his chickens. Archie put down his pencil and paused again, looking over his little flock. Tom had said simple commands worked best. It felt a bit silly, thinking of commands for chickens. He thought about the most common commands for dogs, like Sit and Stay and Quiet. That wasn't much help - none of them sounded like anything that would elicit extraordinary behaviour from his chickens.

Archie absently plucked a few blades of grass and tossed them one by one into the air, the chickens darting forward as they fell then turning away with disinterest once they realised it was just grass.

Finally, he picked up his pencil and started scribbling away on his notepad. When he'd finished, it read:

Lola - SHIELD

Olive - WHISTLE

Rosie - GROW

Coco - SPEED

Milk and Sugar -

70

His pencil hovered over the blank space next to the names of his two smallest chickens. When he had first discovered the chickens' extraordinary talents, his two silkie chickens were the exception. The Smalls hadn't shown any sign of special abilities at all. They'd just stood off to the side, looking small and puffy and somewhat bemused. He didn't know what their powers were, or if they even had powers. In truth, Archie wasn't even convinced that they could properly hear or see anything at all with those giant balls of puffiness on their heads. Nonetheless, Archie felt he should have a command for them, if only to complete his list. In the end he settled on SMALL PUFFS, which seemed like more of a cutesy nickname than a command, but couldn't think of anything else that fit.

With a flame of determination in his belly and his pockets stuffed with grated cheese, Archie stood up and faced his chickens.

He clapped his hands and clucked his tongue to call them over. Immediately, all six members of the little flock raised their heads and ambled over towards him. They gathered around him expectantly.

71

This is off to a good start, thought Archie. *They're actually listening!*

Feeling a bit foolish, Archie spoke to his chickens.

"Okay girls. I don't know if you can understand me... but I'm going to try anyway. Here goes. I'm going to ask each of you to do something. Ok?"

Four pairs of eyes and two motionless pom pom heads stared blankly back at him.

Archie felt even more foolish, but he took a deep breath and kept going.

"So, if you can understand me, please, PLEASE, follow my commands - I've got cheese for you as a reward. See?" He dipped his hand into his pocket and pulled out a few shreds of cheese.

The appearance of cheese had definitely attracted their attention. At the mention of "Cheese" all six pairs of eyes brightened with interest, the silkies tilting their heads to give Archie a rare glimpse of their tiny faces.

Archie faced Coco. He squeezed his hand tightly, moulding the loose shreds of cheese into a small lump.

"Ok. You first Coco - SPEED!" he said firmly and he threw a wad of cheese as far as he could.

There was a sudden flash of movement and a fluttering of breeze in Coco's vacant space, the air suspended like a ghostly shadow left behind. Another ripple of air streaked across the yard, trailed by a line of lightly smoking grass and dancing leaves, and Coco's beak closed on the cheese just as it hit the ground.

Archie blinked and suddenly Coco was back in front of him, a satisfied look on her face.

"Coco - SPEED!" he said again, throwing the cheese behind him. Archie felt the air swirl around his legs as Coco flashed past him, snapped the cheese out of the air and returned to her original position before he had time to even turn his head. The air held the faint whiff of smoke from several scorch marks on the grass.

"YES!" he yelled, punching the air in triumph.

Grinning wildly, Archie stooped and swiftly scooped up Rosie.

"You next, Rosie girl," he told her. Tucked under his right arm like a fat, ruffled football, Rosie fluffed out her feathers and growled at him. He reached awkwardly into his pocket with his free hand and retrieved a squashed lump of cheese. Archie held the cheese in front of Rosie and said firmly, "Okay Rosie. GROW!"

Rosie stretched out her neck, growling and reaching for the cheese.

"Rosie, GROW!" Archie repeated, continuing to hold the cheese just out of reach.

Rosie's growls increased in volume. Her puffy feathers ruffled in indignation. Archie gasped as his arm suddenly shifted and he felt Rosie swelling, her body ballooning into a huge, giant hulk of a chicken. He struggled and tilted to the side, straining to hold the huge weight. Unable to hold her one-handed any longer, Archie awkwardly tucked his left arm under the giant feathered mass that Rosie had become.

Seizing her opportunity, Rosie swivelled her head and deftly pecked the cheese from Archie's left hand. As she gobbled up the treat Archie felt Rosie soften under his arm. Her giant bulk was becoming smaller and smaller and almost as swiftly as she had grown Rosie was back to her normal size.

"Amazing! Rosie, you wonderful chicken!" exclaimed Archie. He stroked Rosie's feathers and gave her a little squeeze.

Feeling almost giddy with excitement, Archie withdrew another handful of cheese from his pocket.

"Rosie, GROW!" he commanded.

Once again, he held the cheese just out of Rosie's reach. And again, he felt her grow and swell and become a huge dead weight under his arm. This time, Archie clutched Rosie with one arm for as long as he could bear, finally releasing her onto the ground with a heavy thud. He raised his cheese hand high into the air, watching in disbelief as Rosie continued to expand in front of him until her outstretched neck and head reached his chest. Her eyes were steely and she growled menacingly as she advanced towards him, her legs solid like tree trunks and tipped with wicked-looking curved claws. Archie swallowed nervously and backed up a few steps.

"Olive, WHISTLE!" said Archie, thrusting his outstretched hand in the direction of the large, black chicken. Olive blinked at him, then opened her beak and began to squawk.

"WHISTLE, Olive, WHISTLE!!" he cried again.

Olive's squawks grew louder, rising in pitch. Archie could feel the unbearable sound coming; he was sure of it. Olive's beak was opened wide - as vast and deep as a black lake - and now she was shrieking. The shrieks became a whistle, shrill and high-pitched. His ears burned.

Archie cried out, "Lola, SHIELD!"

The whistling was unbearably piercing and as he slapped his hands to his ears he opened his fingers and flung the cheese at Lola. There was a *schwing* sound of steel slicing through air. Hands clutched to his ears and eyes screwed up in pain, Archie saw Lola's wings snap out in front of her, the flying cheese deflecting off the wing-shield and scattering across the yard.

76

Almost immediately the chickens transformed. Olive's beak snapped shut and the ear piercing whistling stopped. She made a beeline for the fallen cheese with Rosie stomping close behind, visibly shrinking as she went. Lola sheathed her wings with a flourish and quickly joined in the cheese hunt.

Archie stood in disbelief, watching the chickens foraging in the grass. He had done it! His commands had actually worked! He had found the secret and discovered the key to unleashing his chickens' superpowers.

As he stood on the grass, still reeling from the enormity of this breakthrough, Archie realised that he had missed something. The tiniest of somethings that he had almost forgotten amidst the chaos of his larger discovery. He crossed the yard to where his two smallest chickens shuffled in unison, their white pom pom heads almost touching.

Crouching down, Archie withdrew a handful of cheese from his pocket and delicately stretched a hand towards the pair. He clucked his tongue softly and spoke quietly to Milk and Sugar.

"Hello there, you two. I almost forgot about you! Let's give this a try."

He showed them the shredded cheese in his hand and said firmly, "Small puffs!"

The silkies stared at him. Nothing happened.

He tried again.

"Small puffs! Uh… go puffs! Puff on! Smalls!"

The feathery pom poms on the heads of the Smalls quivered. Archie held his breath. The air around him felt dense and too tight. His outstretched hand was trembling and he forced himself to hold it steady.

Then, after the longest of moments in which Archie thought his chest must surely explode from the tension, the Smalls stretched their necks and… stepped forward to peck the cheese from Archie's hand.

Archie exhaled slowly, the tightness draining from his chest. He stroked the fluffy white backs of Milk and Sugar as they ate, marvelling at the softness of their feathers and their extreme level of cuteness. When they had finished the cheese, the Smalls lifted their tiny faces and murmured soft, melodic clucks to each other.

Archie gently scooped up both silkies and held them close to his face. They were so small he could hold the two of them in his cupped hands. He whispered to them, "I don't know if you do have powers. But it doesn't matter. You're special anyway."

He gave them a little squeeze before depositing them onto the grass. Then he picked up his notebook and pencil and, smiling to himself, he turned and went back into the house.

Chapter Nine: Sweets And Secrets

Buoyed by his success with the chickens, Archie returned to school with a new spring in his step. He joined the lunchtime scrambles with his friends with renewed energy, the secret of his super-chickens burning inside like a glowing ember. Everything seemed lighter, easier. He was happy and carefree, his previous worries about evil groundskeepers and secret plans fading from his mind as school life continued to move forward.

There had been further discussions about the upcoming School Fete. Archie's teacher had announced that their class would be running a Lucky Spin stall, with a giant spinning wheel and bags of sweets and lollies as prizes. It would cost participants $1 for a turn on the Lucky Spin wheel, with prizes awarded for spins landing on winning numbers. They had all been given notes to take home to their parents, calling for lolly donations and volunteers to run the stall.

Archie's friend Ryan had told him and Josh that his class was going to be selling ice-cream spiders at the Fete. And Ryan had heard from his older sister that there would be a food van selling hot chips AND Dagwood dogs AND fairy floss. Everyone was beyond excited, a buzz of anticipation humming around the school at breaks and between classes. Even the teachers seemed to be swept up in the undercurrent of excitement, though they mostly tried not to show it.

That week, Archie and Josh had been designated for tuckshop duty. Just before the bell rang signalling the start of first break, the two boys were dispatched ahead of the rest of the class. They headed towards the undercover tuckshop area and lined up with other pairs of students, each waiting for their turn to collect the tuckshop order tray for their class.

"Did your mum order you anything today?" Josh asked Archie.

"No, Dad packed my lunch today. Mum normally only orders me tuckshop when it's pizza and ice cream day and then only if I remember to tell her. You?"

Josh shook his head. "Nope. Just sandwiches. Ham and cheese I think." He continued to enthusiastically describe the contents of his lunchbox, Archie only half listening as Josh prattled on.

The tuckshop area was relatively quiet, as only a handful of designated class pairs were waiting to receive their class orders. The tuckshop wouldn't open to the rest of the student body for another ten minutes, after the allocated eating time was finished and students were free to play. Then the area was busy, filled with kids lining up with handfuls of change and eager to snap up packets of chips and chocolates and icy-poles.

Josh had now moved on to listing things that he would DEFINITELY put in his lunchbox if it were up to him. The contents of his ideal lunchbox seemed to be drawn solely from the exceedingly long list of Josh's favourite chips, chocolate biscuits and sweets.

They had moved up a couple of places in the short line and Archie could now see into the kitchen area at the back of the tuckshop. He spotted the head tuckshop lady, Ms Dibblehuff, shuffling around near a large steel sink where several large pots sat upturned. She was a short, squat woman and wore a checkered apron stretched tightly across her ample middle and tied in a tight bow at the small of her back. A hairnet on her head enclosed a mop of mousy brown hair flecked with grey.

With her short temper and beady stare, the head tuckshop lady was almost as intimidating as the school groundskeeper. Normally she kept to the back of the tuckshop kitchen and only rarely served students at the front counter. This area was manned by a rotation of younger, more friendly tuckshop staff.

Ms Dibblehuff had been known to glare and snap at students for the smallest of transgressions.

Paying with too many small coins. Paying with a note larger than ten dollars. Stuttering when placing an order. Saying your order too quietly. Saying your order too loudly. Ordering more than one item.

Or the worst crime of all - forgetting it was Wednesday and not Tuesday and ordering a cheeseburger instead of a hot dog and then having to endure the humiliation of being told off in front of everyone because, "TODAY is WEDNESDAY and cheeseburgers are only served on TUESDAY and DON'T YOU EVEN KNOW THE DAYS OF THE WEEK, YOU SILLY LITTLE CHILD??"

This last incident had actually happened to one of Josh's big sisters' friends and served only to make Archie, Josh and all the other kids more terrified of the head tuckshop lady.

Archie quickly averted his eyes in case

Ms Dibblehuff looked over. He did NOT want to be caught staring.

Out of the corner of his eye, Archie saw a figure in navy blue step in through the back door of the tuckshop kitchen area.

Archie watched as the head tuckshop lady wandered over to the navy blue man, his tall frame leaning against the steel bench. She lifted her chin at Mr Franksman by way of a greeting and squinted her piggy little eyes at him.

"Ms Dibblehuff," said the groundskeeper. "How is everything?"

"Good, good..." replied the head tuckshop lady. "You?"

Mr Franksman shrugged noncommittally.

Ms Dibblehuff gave a tiny grunt. "Just finished the plans for our stall at the Fete. We usually sell plenty of drinks and chips, plus a bit of hot food - but that's mainly the adults really. Good for the till, not so good for the clean up mind you."

She tutted and shook her head before continuing.

"Yes, the kids all load up on sugar and snacks and then run off and fling their rubbish all around the grounds. Dirty little rats."

Mr Franksman's eyes narrowed. "I know EXACTLY what you mean. They ARE just like nasty little rats if you ask me. Scurrying around everywhere and making a disgusting mess."

He paused, glancing around as if expecting to see rats descending upon the kitchen at that very moment.

"And this Fete business is the worst of all!" he continued. "The place is left in a complete disgrace - grounds trampled, grass ruined, rubbish everywhere! All my hard work keeping everything neat and clean just ruined."

Ms Dibblehuff nodded sympathetically. "Yes, it's a shame, all the mess left behind. Such a lot of work. But there's nothing to be done, I'm afraid. Fete night has always been so popular. It'll keep running for a long time."

Mr Franksman's thin lips pressed together, a sinister smile stretching across his face.

"Oh, you never know, Ms Dibblehuff. Just because it's been this way for a long time doesn't mean it will always stay the same. There's always a chance that it could be cancelled."

His face turned hard and his eyes glinted as he finished cryptically, "A lot can go wrong with a big event like this. You just never know what could happen.."

He gave Ms Dibblehuff a brisk nod as she wiped her hands on her apron and began drying a large silver pot with a cloth. Then he turned on his heel and strode off, unaware of the small boy standing just a few metres away with ears burning and eyes as wide as saucers.

Archie watched him go, his mouth hanging open in disbelief. He had heard the whole thing.

Chapter Ten: Strike One

Walking back to their classroom with the tuckshop tray, Archie turned and hissed to Josh, "Did you hear what Mr Franksman said? *A lot can go wrong with a big event like this. You just never know what could happen.*"

He paused to allow these words to sink in before plowing on determinedly.

"He's plotting something. I just know he is!"

Josh scoffed at this. "Archie, come on! He's just a cranky old man who doesn't like people messing up his grounds. It's not like he's actually going to DO anything about it."

Archie gave Josh a look that said, *really?*

Josh gave Archie a look back that said, *yeah, really*.

"Dude! He may be a bit scary and cranky and stuff. But he's not, like, some evil villain with crazy schemes! Not for real life."

Archie frowned. "Ok. Fine. You can think that, but I still think he's up to something… and I've got a plan on how to suss out EXACTLY what that is. Will you at least help me with that?"

Josh rolled his eyes, but listened as Archie quickly whispered his idea.

After the bell had rung for play time the two boys quickly made their way through the school, coming to a halt at a low chain-link fence. Beyond the fence stood a solitary building, old fence palings leaning up against its sides and stacks of grey pavers heaped around randomly like discarded dominoes. On one side of the building a pair of roller doors stared at them like a winking face, one roller door raised, the other closed shut. Beyond the open roller door the boys could see clearly into the spacious shed, where tools hung neatly along one side wall and various machinery sat parked in a row.

Archie noted the space between a four-wheeled ATV and a small push mower, which stood out like a gap toothed smile. He looked around in satisfaction.

"Ok. We know that Mr Franksman is out on the oval with the big mower, so he should be busy for a while. I'll sneak into the shed and have a look around. You stay here and if you see any teachers coming just make a loud bird noise to warn me. I'll take this football with me so if anyone comes I can say I was just in here to get the ball back. Ok?"

Josh nodded vigorously. Then he frowned.

"What kind of bird noise should I make?"

"What?" said Archie.

"What kind of bird noise should I make? You know, so you know it's me, and not like, an actual bird for real life."

"Seriously?"

"Yeah, we need to pick a bird," stated Josh matter-of-factly. "Um. Pigeons are too quiet. Maybe a kookaburra? No wait - how about a plover? Yeah, a plover! Ert ert ert ert ert! They even sound like an alarm. That's it. I'm a plover!"

Josh looked extremely pleased with himself.

"Go on! You go check it out. Plover-Josh has got your back. Ert ert ert ert!!"

Archie gave him a look of disbelief, but eventually said, "Fine. You be a plover. Just make sure you're keeping a lookout. Don't get, like... distracted and stuff."

Grinning widely, Josh gave Archie a double thumbs up as he scrambled over the fence, jogged towards the shed and through the open roller door.

It took a few moments for his eyes to adjust to the dim light inside.

He looked around, scanning the room for anything unusual. At first glance everything appeared to be in order. The shed was neat and tidy, as he had expected. All the tools seemed to be in their place, hanging on the wall or on hooks attached to the large pinboard above a workbench.

Then Archie noticed a small area partitioned off from the rest of the shed. He poked his head around the thin wall divider and gave a sharp intake of breath. The small, cramped space contained a small desk strewn with papers. And tucked in beside the desk like a broody hen was a battered old oven draped with a faded blue towel. Archie's eyes swam over the scene. This had to be the oven-machine from the forest! He lifted the towel gingerly and took in the extra panel on the top, a series of complicated wires poking out and connecting to the back of the oven-machine.

Archie recalled the afternoon he had spied Mr Franksman with the oven-machine. The top panel had flashed brightly, numbers splashed across a screen as the oven-machine whirred and hummed. Now the maze of buttons and lights on its surface sat dark and still, the oven-machine silent and brooding.

Not daring to touch anything, Archie replaced the towel and turned his attention to the papers on the desk. He leafed through pages quickly, taking in a detailed design drawing of the oven-machine and its control panel and something that looked like coding instructions.

His chest seemed to turn to ice as his eyes roved over the next few pages. There was a map of the school Fete layout and an event run sheet with a series of actions listed out against times with military precision. Words jumped out at him from the pages like hastily issued threats.

OPERATION JURASSIC INCURSION.

Initiate time sequence.

Activate interspatial portal.

Execute dinosaur incursion protocol.

Archie's head swam as he tried to take it all in. He could not make sense of everything, but there was no mistaking the bold print encircled in red at the bottom of the final page.

FETE CANCELLED.

Archie had seen enough. Replacing the papers back on the desk as best as he could, he hastily left the shed.

Josh was shuffling around by the fence, his arms folded like wings at his side as he swivelled his head and chirped to himself.

"Josh! You'll never believe what I just saw -" Archie started to say, as he scrambled back over the fence.

Josh cut him off. "Ert ert! I'm not Josh, I'm PLOVER-JOSH! Ert ert ert ert!"

"Omigod. You're such an idiot."

Josh just grinned at him. "Anyway, we'd better hurry. The bell literally rang like a minute ago."

As they made their way back to the classroom, Archie told Josh what he'd found in Mr Franksman's shed.

Suddenly Archie stopped and slapped a hand to his head.

"Oh no. The ball! I put it down when I was looking through stuff. I left it in the shed!" he groaned.

"You go on - I've got to get it out of there or he'll know someone has seen his plans!"

He sprinted back the way they'd come and vaulted over the fence, barely pausing to check if anyone was around. Then he darted through the open roller door and grabbed the ball from the floor next to the oven-machine. His feet pounded on the path all the way to the classroom. Heart hammering in his chest, Archie quickly stuffed the ball into his bag on the rack. He darted into the classroom and slid into the chair behind his desk, panting. His teacher was writing on the board, her back to the class. Hope soared within him as he thought he'd done it. He was in the clear! And then plummeted when, without turning around, Miss Mitchum spoke.

"Archie. You're late. That's a red strike for you."

Chapter Eleven: Archie Shares His Discovery

It was some time before Archie and Josh had a chance to get together and properly discuss what Archie had discovered in Mr Franksman's shed. Their hastily whispered conversations in class had not gone down well. Archie could swear Miss Mitchum had eyes in the back of her head, not to mention supersonic hearing. His teacher had stemmed their discussions almost before they began, finally separating the pair of them and threatening to give them both red strikes.

Eventually they got their chance to talk, away from the watchful eyes and eavesdropping of their teacher.

Josh rounded on Archie. "Dude! I know you already told me what you saw in that shed. But are you like, TOTALLY sure? What if those plans are for, like, some weird creepy game or show at the Fete? You know, like the Halloween Disco haunted house? How do you know it's for real and not like... a joke or something?"

Archie shook his head. "No. This can't be any kind of joke, the plans were WAY too detailed. I thought I was going crazy before, but I'm SURE this is for real."

He glanced at Josh again before continuing. "Plus, there's more to it. I didn't tell anyone before because, well, I didn't think anyone would believe me. But after all I've seen and heard now, I KNOW this is the real deal."

He filled Josh in on everything that he had seen in the forest at the edge of the school. Mr Franksman tinkering with the strange oven-machine. The eerie swirling portal. And of course, the unforgettable noise of some horrifying creature sounding as if it were about to burst out of the swirling depths and destroy them all.

Josh gave a low whistle. "Wow. Seriously. Just... WOW! A time portal? And dinosaurs? I know you were suss on Mr Franksman before, but this... this is next level crazy!"

He shook his head in disbelief.

"The Fete is next week. What are we going to do about it?"

"Well. I have a plan. Actually, it's more like a Plan A and a Plan B," said Archie. "Plan A is to sneak into the shed again and try to sabotage the machine. And if that doesn't work - well, Plan B is to stop him from using the machine on the night of the Fete."

Josh looked doubtful.

"I mean, this is a seriously crazy situation," said Josh with a worried frown. "What if we get there and it turns out he's actually some kind of super villain? We're just kids!"

"Actually, there's something else I need to tell you," Archie said.

He paused for the smallest of moments.

"We might just be kids, but I've got some... friends... who might be able to help us."

"Right. Great!" said Josh. "Who are these friends? Do I know them?"

"Well. You kind of do. But not exactly. You know them but you also don't know them, just like I know them but didn't really know them until... I found out what I now know about them…" Archie finished lamely.

"Archie. You are making no sense. Less than no sense! How can I know them but not know them?" Josh exclaimed.

Archie held up his hands, conceding defeat. "Ok. Ok. Sorry! I'll tell you."

He took a deep breath. "It's my chickens. They're not just chickens. They have special powers."

Josh looked momentarily lost for words.

"Chickens," he said eventually.

"Yes. My chickens."

"And they have… powers?"

"That's right. Super powers. Like superheroes."

"So… super chickens?"

"Yes. I guess they are. The Super Chickens."

They both paused, Archie watching Josh nervously to try and gauge his reaction. Josh's brow was deeply furrowed and he looked like he was thinking extremely hard.

Finally, he looked at Archie and spoke. "That. Is. Awesome! Super chickens! How did you not tell me about this before?!"

"Well, I -" Archie started, but Josh cut him off.

"SO awesome! Chickens with super powers! Superhero chickens! Or are they more like mutant chickens?"

"Well, they -"

"No, wait - what if one of the mutant chickens pecks you or something - will you get super chicken powers too? Or become part super chicken? What if

100

you already ARE part super chicken? Omigod that would be AWESOME. You can be Chook Man. No - Cluck Boy! Wait, I've got it. The Incredible Rooster!"

"Um... what??"

"Yeah! The Incredible Rooster and his band of Super Chickens! And I can be your faithful sidekick, Plover Josh!" Josh grinned. "Or, you know, I can be your guy in the chair!"

"My guy in the chair??"

"Yeah, the guy in the chair. You know, I can wear a headset and you can have an earpiece and I can radio in and tell you where you need to be and stuff. On your mission. As The Incredible Rooster. With the Super Chickens."

Now it was Archie's turn to look lost for words.

When he finally spoke again, he chose his words carefully. He didn't want to crush Josh's enthusiasm, just maybe tone it down a little.

"Um. Thanks. I mean, thanks for getting on board with all of... this. And for believing me. But I don't have any special chicken powers. It's just the chickens. They DO have powers, I've seen them. And

I've been training them to respond to special commands."

"Dude. Still awesome! Though I am a bit disappointed you don't have super chicken powers. You can still call yourself The Incredible Rooster if you want though."

"Um, thanks?" said Archie. "I guess you can still be the guy in the chair?"

"Yes! This is going to be AWESOME. I won't let you down, Incredible Rooster!" declared Josh. "Now. Tell me all about these super chickens of yours and what they can do and more importantly, how you get them to do it."

So just like they were brainstorming ideas for a school project, Archie and Josh put their heads together and worked on their plan. They went over every little detail Archie could think of about the super chickens and the groundskeeper and the Fete, until Josh knew everything Archie knew, and Archie began to feel just a tiny bit like The Incredible Rooster, and Josh most definitely felt like Plover Josh, the Guy in the Chair.

Chapter Twelve: Strike Two

Archie and Josh lingered on the footpath, where they had a good view of both Mr Franksman's shed and a corner of the school oval. They had both agreed that Archie would sneak into the shed with Josh posted on lookout, just as they had done last time. Now Archie stared at the shed with a sense of giddy anticipation, determined that this time he would not just be a passive witness to the groundskeeper's sinister plans. This time, he resolved to make a difference, to damage the machine enough that the plan could not go ahead.

Under one arm he held a football - a key component of their cover story should they get caught - and in his other hand he clutched a small tool case. Just like last time, the boys had waited until they were sure the groundskeeper was busy mowing, checking that the big mower was absent from the line of machinery parked just inside the open roller door of the shed.

"Okay dude. Good to go?" whispered Josh.

"Yep. All good," Archie whispered back.

"Cool. Now remember, you want to try to unscrew the control panel and strip the casing off some wires before cutting them."

"Ok."

"But not too much! You want the damage to be small and tricky to spot, to make it harder to fix."

"Got it."

"No, you should say Roger That. It sounds better."

"What?"

"You know. For the mission. As the Incredible Rooster."

Archie looked at Josh incredulously. "Does it really matter?"

Josh considered this for a moment.

"Well, yeah, it does. I mean, what if I'm listening to you through my headset and you say 'got it' but I hear 'not it'? Or 'rotted'? Or 'God did?' Or 'pot lid'?"

"But you're not even wearing a headset! And why would I say pot lid??"

Josh shrugged. "Dunno. Maybe I'm the guy in the chair who also cooks."

Archie couldn't think of a single thing to say in response to this.

Instead he asked, "Also, why are we whispering when there's nobody around... and there's a very loud lawn mower mowing very loudly?"

Josh rolled his eyes. "Duh. Because this is a TOP SECRET mission and on top secret missions EVERYBODY whispers. It makes everything seem, you know, more mysterious and secretive and stuff."

"O-kaay.."

"Anyway. I have to save my voice in case I need to sound the plover-alarm," whispered Josh matter-of-factly. "But enough about me - we have the all clear, Houston you are cleared for take-off."

"I'm confused. Is this a top secret mission or a space launch??"

"No time for questions! Go go go!"

Josh waved his hands impatiently, hustling Archie over the chain-link fence towards the shed. This time Archie bolted into the shed without hesitation. He moved quickly past the parked machinery towards the partitioned off area, his heart drumming inside his chest. He was already visualizing the task ahead, his hands moving automatically to retrieve things from the small tool bag. Archie darted into the makeshift office area behind the partition and immediately his heart sank. The desk was neat and clear of papers, the small space beside it empty. Quickly he scanned around the rest of the shed, hoping to spot the now familiar old oven tucked into some dark corner, draped in the faded blue towel. But it was no good. The oven-time-machine was nowhere to be seen.

Grimly he retraced his steps back to where Josh stood on watch. He dropped the ball and tool bag over the fence at his friend's feet.

"It's not there," said Archie, clambering back over the fence. "The machine is gone. He must have moved it already."

"Oh no," Josh groaned. "Where is it now?"

"I don't know. Maybe he's shifted it to the forest where it was last time. Maybe it's already set up and he's ready to activate it."

Archie picked up the ball and thrust it into Josh's arms. "Quick. We've still got time if we hurry."

The two boys sprinted towards the oval.

As they ran, Archie breathlessly outlined his plan to Josh. "Ok. I'm going to go into the forest and see if I can find the machine. You run around here and if someone's coming or the bell rings, kick the ball as close to the forest as you can and make your bird noise to warn me to come back."

When they reached the trees at the edge of the oval Archie did not stop running. Without so much as a backwards glance, he sprinted straight for the thick cluster of trees at the far side of the oval.

Pausing briefly to catch his breath, Josh watched his friend racing across the green expanse of the oval. "Good luck and godspeed, Incredible Rooster," he whispered, saluting the small figure as it disappeared into the trees. "It's up to you now, Plover Josh. You're the eyes and ears on the ground from here on."

He dropped the ball to the ground and stopped it with his foot, then began to dribble the ball around rather clumsily. Every now and then he would stop and swivel his head around, his arms folded sharply at his sides as he made soft plover noises.

A couple of younger boys he didn't recognize wandered over and gestured at the ball. "Hey. Do you want to play a game?"

Josh raised his arms with his thumbs held out, like the spurs on a plover's wings. Screeching shrilly he swooped towards the boys, sending them stumbling backwards with yells of shock. As the younger boys turned to make a swift exit Josh could hear them muttering "what a weirdo" and "could have just said no". He grinned to himself.

As he was completing his plover victory dance, bobbing and strutting triumphantly around the ball, he heard it. The melodic chiming of the end-of-break bell rang out from the nearby school buildings. Josh immediately ceased his dance. He drew his leg back, ready to kick the ball as hard as he could.

But before he could even get a touch on it, the teacher on duty called out to him. "Lunch break is over! The bell has gone, grab your ball and head back in please. You don't want to be late for assembly."

The plover warning in the back of his throat shrinking, Josh reluctantly headed off the oval and back into the school. When he reached the buildings he turned around to look forlornly at the far forest. There was no sign of Archie. He had no way to warn him that break was over. Without the ball, he would have no excuse for being late. As he made his way back to the classroom Josh felt sick inside knowing his friend would have no idea of the trouble facing him on his return.

Oblivious to anything going on in the rest of the school, Archie moved quickly through the trees towards the small clearing. The light was brighter within the forest than it had been the last time he'd ventured inside. With each branch he pushed aside, each tree he rounded, the memories came flooding back. Then suddenly, he was there. This time standing behind the small shrub instead of crouching down low in fearful silence. He looked over the clearing. Empty. Quickly he hurried into the middle of the open space, looking around wildly in search of the oven-machine, but there was no sign of it.

After searching behind trees and shrubs surrounding the clearing, Archie paused. He stood with his hands on his head, listening intently for any noises or alarms above the quiet forest sounds.

Realizing that he had now spent considerable time in the forest and was yet to hear a sound from Josh, Archie abandoned his futile efforts, cursing softly under his breath as he retraced his steps. As he emerged from the trees Archie looked out over the empty oval. There was no sign of Josh or any other students.

A horrible sinking feeling swelled in his stomach as it dawned on him that something must have gone terribly wrong. He broke into a run.

The rest of his class was already filing into the undercover area for assembly, Miss Mitchum at the head of the winding crocodile of students. Archie quickly joined the end of the line, hoping desperately that she would not notice his late arrival.

He increased his pace and shuffled his way up through the pairs of his classmates until he was walking in stride with Josh. The crocodile had almost come to a halt, its segments slowing and condensing as the line filed in straight behind another seated class.

Just as Archie almost dared to hope that he had gotten away with it, Miss Mitchum once again spoke to him without breaking stride or turning around.

"That's the second time you've been late coming back in after lunch, Archie. Another red strike. And I'm afraid if there are any more infringements like this I will have no choice but to contact your parents about your disappointing behaviour."

Chapter Thirteen: Strike Three

Sitting cross-legged at assembly, Archie and Josh exchanged meaningful looks. Josh mouthed *sorry* to him. Archie opened his mouth to share his discovery, or rather, his lack of discovery, but Josh gave a little shake of his head and mouthed *not now*. Talking during assembly was strictly forbidden.

In front of the school assembly Mr Johnsson, the school principal, was standing behind a lectern and speaking into the microphone. His voice crackled slightly over the speakers as he called for the students to stand for the singing of the national anthem.

As the whole school got to their feet, the two boys used the noisy commotion as an opportunity to exchange fast, desperate whispers.

"Archie, what happened? Did you find it?" hissed Josh.

"No! It wasn't there. I couldn't find anything!"

113

"Where is it then?"

"I don't know! He must have moved it somewhere else."

The finishing bars of the anthem came to an end, followed by another brief hum of activity as the students were re-seated.

"What are we going to do? Do we push on with Plan A?" Josh whispered.

"I don't know. I need to think!" Archie hissed back.

Mr Johnsson ran through a series of announcements, including congratulating several students on their various sporting achievements and thanking all the students who had collected trash from the area outside class 1H.

Archie and Josh were only half listening, their minds elsewhere.

Mr Johnsson moved on to speaking about the Fete, reminding everyone that it was on that weekend.

The two boys sat up a little straighter and pricked up their ears.

"Just a reminder to all students that the oval will be out of bounds for the entire day tomorrow. There will be contractors setting up the amusement rides and our wonderful staff and volunteers will be busy erecting marquees for the stalls," said Mr Johnsson. "The out of bounds zone includes the football pitch and the trees bordering the oval. We don't want anyone getting in the way or getting hurt so please just keep clear of that whole area."

Archie and Josh exchanged dark looks. This was not good news.

"And last but not least," Mr Johnsson continued. "A huge thank you to our groundskeeper, Mr Franksman, for the wonderful job he has done in preparing the grounds. They are looking fantastic - an absolutely top notch effort just in time for the Fete. I'm sure it will be an amazing night for all. Let's have a round of applause for Mr Franksman."

As Mr Johnsson led the applause, the two boys swivelled their heads around, searching for the groundskeeper amongst the school staff and teachers. They spotted him at the side of the undercover area, leaning against a pole with his arms folded across his chest and a strange, smug smile on his face. He gave a brief nod and raised a hand to acknowledge the applause.

As the clapping died down and the principal moved onto the next item on the agenda, Archie held his gaze on Mr Franksman. The smile on his face had grown wider, but this did not make him look warm and friendly. His thin lips spreading across his teeth in a sort of grimace made him look even more sinister.

Archie felt an icy chill creep over him at the sight of that cold smiling face. Could they not see what he saw? Why did nobody else suspect him?

He leaned his head towards Josh. "It's too late for Plan A now. We don't have time to try and find the machine before tomorrow and anyway, the whole school is going to be swarming with people. There's no chance of doing anything without being caught. So that settles it. We have to move to Plan B."

Too busy watching the smiling groundskeeper, Archie and Josh completely forgot about the eagle eyes of Miss Mitchum and failed to notice as she quietly stepped down the line of her class.

They were still whispering frantically when they both felt a tap on the shoulder as Miss Mitchum addressed the pair of them. "Archie. Josh. Separate!" she hissed, her voice low and furious. "Josh - you stay here. Archie - over there, next to me where I can keep an eye on you." She glared at the two boys. Archie guiltily stood up and slunk over to the end of line next to Miss Mitchum's low chair.

"And that's another red strike for you Archie. I did warn you. Your parents will be hearing from me this afternoon."

Sure enough, when Archie's mum arrived to pick him up from school, he was met with a look of stony faced disappointment. His dad, who would normally still be at work at this time, had evidently been summoned to the meeting as well. He too looked equally disappointed.

As his parents followed a grim looking Miss Mitchum into the classroom, Archie sat down outside on a hard wooden bench. He stared dolefully at his shoes, his legs kicking slowly against the wall behind him in despair. He had a feeling his parents would not take this well.

When the meeting between Miss Mitchum and his parents was finally over, the sad little trio made their way to the car. Archie climbed silently into the backseat, slinging his bag onto the seat beside him. The car doors closed with a decisive thud, loud against the stony silence. It gave Archie the feeling of being locked in a tomb. Archie's mum turned and rounded on him almost immediately.

"Do you want to explain to us what's been going on?"

Archie took a deep breath and the words began to spew out of him. He tried to explain about the groundskeeper's scheming, the time machine and dinosaurs returning from the past and it all being a crazy plan to stop the Fete. But it was no good. His mum held up her hand and cut him off mid sentence.

"That's enough, Archie!" she declared. "Look, I don't know where you get these ideas from. Is it those comic books you've been reading, or something on

TV? First this idea about the chickens behaving strangely and now you've concocted the notion of some... some crazy plot at school?"

His mum gave a great sigh and her voice softened slightly. "It's great that you've got such an active imagination Archie, it really is. But you just can't let it get in the way of following the rules and doing the right thing at school."

She paused and shared a look with Archie's dad that parents only use when they are about to share really unwelcome information.

"We really didn't want to do this, because we know how much you've been looking forward to this weekend - but you've given us no choice. So your Dad and I have made a decision. You are officially grounded, starting from now. Which means you won't be going to the Fete tomorrow night."

Archie opened his mouth to protest, but simply could not find any words. He closed his mouth with a sigh, turning and gazing out the window in despair. This was an absolute disaster.

Chapter Fourteen: The Lowest Point

Archie didn't speak to his parents the whole way home. Staring out the car window as they sped past trees and houses, he wondered how the plan had managed to go so wrong. When their car finally pulled into the driveway and the engine switched off, the stony silence lingered in the air like a bad smell.

Archie hung his school bag on its hook and headed straight for his room, dumping his lunch bag and water bottle in the kitchen on his way. Halfway to his room he changed his mind, turned on his heel and headed out into the backyard, head down and feeling sorry for himself.

Immediately, the chickens trotted across the lawn towards him.

"Hi girls," he said sadly. "I hope you've all had a better day than I have."

The girls clucked at him softly, all except Lola quickly losing interest after seeing that he had nothing for them. He picked Lola up and stroked her smooth brown feathers. Something about holding a chicken made everything feel just the tiniest bit better.

Over the fence he spotted his neighbour, Tom, holding the garden hose in one hand. Tom's little dog, Nick Furry, was trotting along behind him like a second shadow. Mouth open and tongue lolling in a wide doggy grin, Nick bounced up and down and yapped.

As Archie watched, Tom spoke to the little dog, smiling. Archie could not hear the words, but it was clear that Nick had heard and understood what was said. He backed up a little way from Tom, his batlike ears quivering as he waited eagerly. Tom adjusted the hose nozzle to a thin stream and flicked the hose so that the water danced in an arc. Nick twisted and jumped, leaping towards the dancing spray. Because of his short legs he could not jump very high, but his ears were pricked and his face a picture of determination. In between leaps he took fast, valiant steps, looking utterly convinced that this time he would most certainly leap high enough to catch the water.

It was quite funny to watch and in spite of his dark mood Archie could not help but smile. Even Lola seemed to be enjoying the show from her higher

122

vantage point tucked under Archie's arm. Her bright eyes followed the movements of the little dog and seemed to sparkle with amusement.

As the elusive dancing water continued to taunt him, Nick's leaps slowed and his enthusiasm waned. Finally, tired out from his efforts, he gave up and lay down on the wet grass, panting.

Tom readjusted the hose to a wider mist and moved towards the vegie patch. He spotted Archie and raised a hand in greeting.

"Hey there Archie!"

"Hi Tom," replied Archie.

"How's the chicken training going?" Tom asked, smiling broadly.

"Oh! Well," said Archie, his cheeks reddening slightly. "Um, the chickens are good! Yeah, they're good." He hadn't really talked about his super chickens to anyone except his best friend Josh.

Tom raised an eyebrow. "Just good?" he teased.

"Um. Yeah. Good."

Archie didn't know what to say. His parents had not believed him and he doubted that even easygoing Tom would take him seriously.

"Doesn't sound like it's good. You don't look very happy."

"It's not that. I... I got in trouble at school. Now I'm grounded," Archie mumbled.

"Oh. I see," said Tom, his smile softening. "Well, these things happen. You just need to remember to keep your head up. Fresh start next week and all that."

Archie didn't answer. The Fete was on tomorrow night. He had not managed to disable the groundskeeper's oven-time-machine. Next week would be too late.

"Well I'll, uh, I'll leave you to it then," Tom said hesitatingly. "Just a word on your chickens though. Even if you're in a bad mood, keep in mind that that's you and not them. It's not their fault. Pets often have a knack for cheering you up if you let them."

When he received no response, Tom gave Archie a sympathetic glance before moving away to water the pumpkin patch.

Archie sat on the grass until the sun had mellowed to buttery warmth, draping the backyard in a soft glow. He thought about his neighbour's parting words. Tom was right, of course, just like he'd been right about the training advice. He may not be able to do anything about the Fete but at least he had his chickens. He could still practice their commands even if there would be no Plan B, no last ditch attempt to foil Mr Franksman's evil plot on the night.

He would just have to pray for the machine to fail somehow, or for some other obstacle to stand in the way and prevent the groundskeeper from carrying out his plan.

Feeling his sense of resolve lifting, he stood up, wiped his hands on his grass-patterned legs and clucked his tongue to call the chickens.

"Girls!" he called. "Come on girls!"

The chickens ambled across the grass towards him.

"Alright. I'm going to get some cheese. Then it's time for practice."

A minute or so later he returned clutching the old green enamel mug, assuming that chickens would recognize and associate it with special treats. He held it up high and addressed the chickens in a firm, clear voice.

"Okay girls! I'm going to run through your commands and ask you to follow them."

Archie showed Coco a piece of cheese. "Coco - SPEED!"

As he threw the cheese he felt the air swirl and a light brown blur shot forward. When Coco returned and stood watching him expectantly he held up a hand.

This time when he gave the command he did not throw anything, but instead simply pointed towards the lemon tree. Coco sped towards the tree, did a lightning fast loop around its base, sped back and then skidded to a halt at Archie's feet.

Archie was ecstatic. He repeated the process with each of his chickens, heaping praise on them after each successful command and rewarding the whole flock with a large handful of cheese from the mug at the end of the session.

*   *   *

Lying in his bed later that night, Archie felt cautiously optimistic. His training session with the chickens had been brilliant. He had tried out all of his commands, first using cheese as a reward and then without.

All of his girls had performed beautifully.

Even Milk and Sugar had seemed to pay extra attention, though they had done no more than sit still and look exceptionally small and cute.

He had done everything he could think of. The chickens were ready. All he could do now was hope for a miracle.

Chapter Fifteen: An Unexpected Visitor

Next morning, sometime after breakfast, there was a knock at the front door. Archie's mum went to answer it. A red bike stood propped up against the wall on the front patio. Standing sheepishly on the doorstep with a backpack slung over one shoulder, was Josh.

Archie's mum looked surprised. "Oh. Hi Josh," she said.

"Hi Archie's mum!" said Josh with a wide, hopeful smile.

"I'm sorry Josh, but Archie's grounded at the moment," said Archie's mum apologetically.

Josh's smile wavered just a fraction. "Um. Yeah, I know. I, uh, overheard my parents saying that Archie wasn't allowed to go to the Fete anymore because he got in trouble at school. And, um... well I just wanted to say that it's kind of my fault too that Archie got three strikes from Miss Mitchum." His face took on a slightly awkward expression.

Archie's mum looked even more surprised. "Oh. Well. That's very good of you to tell us, Josh."

Josh cleared his throat and plowed on determinedly. "See, I was supposed to let Archie know if the bell rang when he was on the oval because he might not hear it, only a teacher made me go back in before I could let him know it had rung, so it was kind of my fault he was late to class. And then I was whispering to him at assembly and he whispered back and so that was kind of both our faults. But probably a bit more my fault because, well, I kind of talk more than Archie does and I'm a bit louder, so it was most likely me that Miss Mitchum heard. But then we both got in trouble anyway because if you've got a red strike the teachers are really on the lookout for any excuse to give you another."

Josh paused, as if appraising what he had just said.

"So anyway, I'm sorry that Archie got in trouble. And that he's going to miss out on the Fete. And I was hoping I could talk to him, since I won't get to see him tonight," he finished, flashing Archie's mum his most winning smile.

By this stage Archie's dad had joined his mum at the front door. They shared a meaningful look, silently considering Josh's request. Then Archie's dad shrugged and said, "I'm fine with that. But I'll leave it up to you, darling." He patted her on the back as he left.

Turning back to Josh, Archie's mum said, "Okay Josh. Since you've made the effort to come over and apologize, I'm happy for you to stay and play with Archie for a bit."

Josh gave a triumphant fist pump and bustled into the house past Archie's mum. With a wry smile, she called after the rapidly retreating form, "Just for an hour or two, ok?"

Archie, who had been eavesdropping on the conversation from the kitchen, gave his best friend a huge grin as Josh bounced in looking like a dog who had just found his favourite toy. The two of them bounded down the hall and into Archie's room, pulling the door firmly shut behind them.

Leaning against the closed bedroom door, Archie let out a low whistle. "Thanks heaps for coming over. I think you really won my mum over with your little speech."

Josh grinned at him. "What can I say? Parents love me!"

He settled himself comfortably on the floor with his back against Archie's bed and began pulling things out of his backpack. Archie watched on with mounting confusion as Josh laid out a ratty brown wig, a fancy dress eagle mask, a box of fart bombs, a pair of walkie talkies, a packet of jelly snakes, a coil of rope, a box containing an impressive looking drone and finally, a multipack of large, brightly coloured girls' underwear.

"Now. We don't have a lot of time, so listen up carefully. You might be grounded, but I've got an idea for Plan C. And just quietly, it is WAY better than your last plans!"

With a final satisfied flourish Josh withdrew a roll of paper from the backpack and spread it out carefully on the floor. It was covered in pencilled sketches and notes. Splashed across the top in large, bold letters was the heading:

Plan C: The Incredible Rooster flies Super Chickens to the Fete by Hen-icopter

"Hen-icopter?" Archie asked incredulously.

"That's right. Hen-icopter. We're going to build it now, so you can get those Super Chickens of yours to the Fete tonight and thwart the evil villain Mr Franksman!"

"You're really onboard with this whole superhero narrative, aren't you?"

"Dude, totally! Oh and sorry about the eagle mask. It was the closest thing to a chicken that I could find," said Josh, picking up the eagle mask and smoothing his thumb over the feathers. "It's for your disguise, by the way - so you don't reveal your secret identity while you're The Incredible Rooster."

"Fair enough," agreed Archie, his eyes roaming over the pile of objects on the floor. "What about the jelly snakes?"

"Well, chickens normally sleep at night, don't they?"

"Um, yeah?" said Archie.

"Well, my mum is always telling me that if I eat too many lollies before bedtime I won't be able to get to sleep for ages. So I figure, before you set off on your mission, you can feed the jelly snakes to the chickens. They'll get a huge sugar rush and then instead of being sleepy, they'll be fully alert and ready to bravely face the evil villain Mr Franksman alongside the fearless Incredible Rooster!"

Archie could not fault the logic in Josh's thinking, so he said nothing. Instead, he grinned at Josh. "Ok. You're a genius. And I'm sure there's a really good reason why you've brought me a whole pack of girl's undies. Now tell me the rest of the plan while we build this hen-icopter."

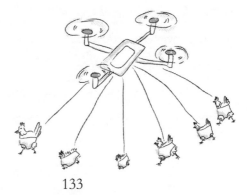

Chapter Sixteen: Plan C

After Josh had left, Archie did his best to conceal his excitement. Even though his insides were positively churning with nervous energy, he did not want to do anything that might arouse suspicion from his parents. He fed the chickens and put away his clean laundry when asked. He helped to set the table for dinner as usual and ate his food calmly and quietly. After dinner, he made a big deal of yawning and rubbing his eyes, before announcing that he was a bit tired from the week and thought he would do some reading before going to bed early. His parents readily accepted this excuse. If anything, they looked pleased that he seemed to have given thought to his actions and was working on turning over a new leaf.

Once alone in his room, Archie sprang into action. He quickly changed out of his pajamas and into a pair of shorts and a dark blue long-sleeved shirt. He checked the contents of his backpack before turning his attention to the bed. After several minutes of activity, he stood back and assessed his handiwork.

Archie had stretched the ratty brown wig over an old football and nestled this into a pillow clad in his pajamas. With the doona cover thrown over the whole lot, the effect was rather convincing - just a glimpse of messy hair and the top sliver of his pajamas. He hoped that once he set off a series of fart bombs in his room, the disgusting smell would be enough to discourage his parents from venturing in close enough to tell it was not really him in the bed at all.

By now the soft light of dusk had all but vanished, with the first evening stars twinkling softly in the sky. Carefully closing the bedroom door, Archie padded silently down the hallway. He inched his head around the corner into the lounge room, noting the two heads of his parents nestled into the back of the couch. He could see a pair of wine glasses on the coffee table. He stood still and watched for a moment. His parents appeared to be totally engrossed in the movie blaring from the TV. From previous experience Archie knew that once settled in like this they were unlikely to stir and would possibly even fall asleep on the couch.

Satisfied, Archie slipped out into the backyard and carefully laid his precious cargo on the grass. Six pairs of brightly patterned undies attached to ropes splayed out around the drone. It looked like a kind of robot insect with multi-coloured wings.

He gathered his chickens from the coop, placing each hen gently by a pair of undies. The chickens were docile and placid, murmuring low clucks at the strangeness of being plucked from their perches in the near darkness. Archie spoke to them reassuringly, asking the girls to trust him and hoping they would understand.

"We've got an important mission, girls. I need your help! So I'm going to strap you all into the hen-icopter and then we'll get underway."

One by one, he fitted each hen snuggly into their undie harness.

When he came to the two silkies, Archie paused. He was still unsure if he should bring them along or not - after all, he didn't even know if they had powers.

Was he putting his two smallest chickens at risk unnecessarily?

"What should I do about you two? You're so small and cute! I really don't want to put you in danger," murmured Archie as he considered the pair.

As if they could sense his hesitation, Milk and Sugar made the decision for him. They stepped forward into their designated pairs of undies, placing their tiny feet through the leg holes and settling down with an air of quiet satisfaction.

Archie could not suppress his grin. The hen-icopter was loaded and ready for take off!

He powered up the drone and immediately the four rotors began rotating with a low-level hum. Archie watched with his heart in his mouth as the hen-icopter slowly began to rise, the harness ropes stretching out until they were taut. Inch by inch it stretched upwards, until the undies were suspended, his chickens tucked into them with their bellies and feet still touching the ground. He slowly pushed the throttle forward and holding his breath, Archie watched as the hen-icopter continued to rise until all six chickens were in the air!

It gave a little shudder as the chickens swayed in their airborne harnesses, then steadied, hovering expectantly above him.

He hoisted his backpack over his shoulders and picked up his bike. Quietly he moved out of the yard, maneuvering the hen-icopter smoothly through the dark sky. He paused for a moment, holding his bike steady as he closed the gate softly behind him.

Hitching his backpack up tighter, Archie swung his leg over his bike, clutching the handlebars with one hand and the hen-icopter remote control in the other. He glanced up at the chickens, hovering above him in their brightly coloured harnesses. They looked calm and alert.

Archie took a deep breath and pulled the eagle mask down over his face. He began pedalling in the direction of the school, the hen-icopter hovering along steadily just in front of him. The feathered tops of the chickens in their patterned undies stood out against the inky darkness like giant incandescent ladybirds.

"Alright. This is it. Time for Plan C!" he said, attempting to motivate himself for what was yet to come. "The Incredible Rooster and the Super Chickens are on their way! Let's go!"

As they moved off down the street and away from the safe haven of his home, Archie could have sworn he saw Lola turn her head back to give him a wink.

Chapter Seventeen: The Confrontation

As Archie neared the school he slowed down, looking around cautiously before continuing. The school car park was full and cars parked nose to tail lined the closest streets. The bike path he had chosen to travel on was dark, quiet and completely deserted. It came to an abrupt end at the edge of a road which bordered the furthest corner of the school. A low chain-link fence ran alongside the road, which Archie knew to be the boundary of the school oval. Beyond the fence a dense cluster of trees loomed over him, tall and ominous in the darkness.

He could hear the muffled sounds of the Fete in the distance; jumbled strands of music mixed with the hum of voices, punctuated with occasional shrieks of children on amusement rides.

With his feet planted on either side of his bike, he carefully navigated the hen-icopter towards a clear space on the tree-lined side of the fence. The chickens clucked nervously as they descended, stretching out their legs and splaying their feet. As they touched solid ground they stepped outwards, the harness attachments spreading out like the tentacles of a bizarre flattened octopus. The whirring hum died down and then ceased as the hen-icopter safely landed. Archie breathed an audible sigh of relief. All of his girls ruffled their feathers and looked around curiously, seemingly waiting for further instructions.

Archie dismounted from his bicycle and leant it against a section of the fence where an unusually tall patch of weeds grew thick and tangled. He tucked a few knotted stems of the straggly plants here and there around the bike and balanced a fallen branch with yellowing leaves on the handlebars. He glanced towards the road and then back at his bike. Finally, satisfied that the bike was sufficiently hidden - at least under the cover of night-time darkness - Archie moved forward and began to unload the chickens.

There was a crackle of static coming from Archie's back.

"...Archie... can you hear me?" came a scratchy voice.

Archie unclipped the walkie-talkie from his back waistband. He pressed the button down and held it to his mouth.

"Josh? I'm at the school, at the fence near the back trees. Where are you?"

"I'm near the food stalls. We got here early because Mum wanted to get a good parking spot."

"Ok. Great. Have you spotted him anywhere? Or the machine? Or seen anything... dodgy?"

"No I haven't seen him, but I did spot something dodgy earlier. And I'm looking at it again right now. Yep, these dagwood dogs are going to be gifts that keep on giving," said Josh.

There was a brief pause. His voice became distinctly muffled as he continued. "Im fapt, I mibe juft hapft do chedk howp dobdgy dey arb..."

"Josh. Are you... eating??" asked Archie. "Seriously? Is now really the time to have a dagwood dog?"

"Wellphfft," came the muffled reply, "issh allff paarb obvf mby cubver. Paarb obvf mby plansh."

Archie took a deep breath and willed himself to not call his best friend an idiot.

"Ok. Fine. Whatever. Eat the dagwood dog. Just... keep looking, okay? Let me know if you spot anything."

"Wodgem dat. Ober am out."

Archie shook his head but he couldn't help grinning just a little. He reclipped the walkie-talkie to his pants waistband and looked around, trying to decide on his next move.

He turned to the chickens, who had gathered close together in a little huddle. Crouching down in front of them and opening his backpack, Archie withdrew the packet of jelly snakes. He fished out a sticky wad of the red and green lollies and offered one to each of the hens in turn. The chickens gobbled them up eagerly.

143

As Archie watched he could see the sugar taking effect, working its way into their bloodstream and doing its work. The chickens were no longer standing and gazing around placidly.

They stretched out their necks and darted their heads this way and that with jerky, agitated movements.

Olive's eyes were bulging even more than usual. The black pupils no longer moved in unison; instead they were dilating and shrinking independently of each other, as though Olive was under the spell of a crazy chicken wizard.

Coco jigged on the spot, her legs moving rapidly in a strange, high-stepping Irish chicken dance. Lola was mechanically swivelling her whole body from side to side in a robotic semicircle, her wings held aloft and snapping into place as she moved.

Rosie seemed undecided on what to do with herself. She kept sitting down with a huff, only to stand back up after several seconds with her front puffed out and neck stretched high. As Archie watched Rosie continued to sit down and stand up. First short. Then tall. Short. Tall. Short. Tall.

Archie found himself rooted to the spot, mesmerized.

Beside Rosie stood the two fluffy white silkies, similarly transfixed by her tall chicken short chicken routine.

Milk and Sugar were completely still except for their pom poms, which quivered up and down in sync with Rosie's movements.

After watching Rosie and the Smalls for what seemed like an eternity, Archie forced himself to snap out of it. With a little shake of his head he came to his senses, shoving a jelly snake in his mouth and stowing the remainder into a pocket of his backpack.

He clapped his hands together briskly.

"Okay super chickens! Time to move! Let's go find this crazy man and his time machine."

He turned on his heel and began to move into the trees, gesturing for the chickens to follow. At a sharp squawk from Lola, the rest of the flock snapped to attention and drew into line. With Lola in the lead they stepped out behind Archie, their jerky movements dulled by shadow as the trees closed around them.

As Archie strode determinedly through the trees his thoughts drifted back to the rough plan that he and Josh had sketched out for the mission. After completing work on the hen-icopter earlier that day, they had spent some time discussing what might happen at the Fete and the roles each of them would play on the night.

Once they had both arrived at the Fete and touched base, Josh would keep a lookout through the school grounds and the Fete itself, while Archie would scout around the forest bordering the school.

They had both agreed that Archie would need to keep out of sight. Firstly because he was, after all, grounded. Josh knew for a fact that his parents would be startled to see Archie out and about and would almost certainly call Archie's parents if he was spotted. The second and more obvious reason for Archie to remain hidden involved his six feathered chicken friends following closely behind him like small, colourful shadows.

"Archie. Think about it," said Josh. "If you stroll into the Fete wearing an eagle mask, flanked by six mutant chickens, I'm pretty sure people are going to notice you. It's not exactly a stealthy entrance, is it?"

"Well, it's not like you're going to have free rein to wander around wherever you like, with your parents and your big sister tailing you!" retorted Archie.

"Don't worry about me! I'll be able to sneak away just fine," grinned Josh. "I've got LOADS of tricks up my sleeve. Plover Josh has got it covered!"

His face turned more serious. "But there's no way you can bring the super chickens into the Fete. Apart from drawing unwanted attention, you don't want them freaking out and making a spectacle of themselves, do you?"

"Yeah ok," said Archie. "Fair point."

"Good. So it's agreed. I'll cover the school buildings and the Fete and you and your feathered friends stick to the forest. We'll use the walkie talkies to keep in touch if either of us spot anything or need help. Ok?"

It had given both boys confidence to lay out their plans and strategies for the mission. When Josh hopped on his bike to ride home, the pair of them parted brimming with optimism, all but convinced that they would succeed.

But outside the comfort and safety of his bedroom, their plans seemed childlike, crude even. Now as he moved forward, the tall, shadowy trees

149

looming over him like sentinels, he felt a pang of fear and wished his friend could be here with him.

Up ahead Archie could see a faint glow of light that seemed to pulse with an unnatural, sinister brightness. Locating a low, bushy shrub, he lifted up a low hanging section and gestured underneath.

"Girls. I'm going to go in closer and investigate. Huddle under here and stay hidden." Archie ushered the chickens into the shelter of the little shrub.

As the chickens shuffled in around the base of the shrub, Archie reached for his walkie-talkie. He pressed the button and spoke into it in a low voice.

"Josh. I think I've found where the oven-time-machine is. I'm going to check it out now. Over."

He waited for Josh to reply but the walkie-talkie remained silent.

Archie tried again. "Josh. Can you hear me? Over."

The walkie-talkie crackled as Josh finally responded, his voice sounding tight and strained.

"Can't talk right now. Good luck Archie. Over."

Josh's reply was muffled amongst a lot of background noise, including what sounded like a cow lowing and water flushing.

Archie decided not to press Josh for details right at that moment. Instead, he crouched down in front of the little flock.

"I'll call out for you if I need you, ok?"

The chickens stared back at him blankly. Olive's pupils danced crazily and her left eye twitched. Lola tilted her head to the side and blinked twice. Rosie ignored him completely, lowering herself to the ground with a huff. He could only just see the Smalls huddled together behind Rosie's puffy backside.

Archie tried again, feeling less certain than before.

"So... if I call out for you, that means I need you to come and help. Ok?"

The chickens continued to stare blankly.

"Uh... right then," Archie finished weakly, not feeling at all confident. "Well, wish me luck!"

Trying to swallow his growing sense of unease, Archie straightened up, a large scraggly branch catching him on the back as he did so. He extracted himself and his backpack from its scratchy tendrils and the shrub quickly righted itself, hiding the chickens from view.

He turned and began to creep towards the glowing light. All too quickly he reached the edge of a small glade where the light seemed to originate from. Archie knelt down and peered through the branches of a low shrub. He looked out into the tiny clearing and instantly his heart sank. The knot of fear twisted inside him and he wished more than ever that he was not alone.

A tall, lanky figure clad in navy blue loomed over the source of the eerie light. The person was bent over a boxy machine on the ground that resembled an old oven. The figure straightened up and the glow from the front panel on the oven-machine illuminated a man's face. It was just as he and Josh had feared. The sharp, angular features of Mr Franksman were clearly visible, his eyes dark and piercing above his tightly drawn mouth.

Archie could see the familiar tool belt looped around the groundskeeper's waist, a set of work gloves and a glasses case clipped to a carabiner. Other than that and the screwdriver held in his hand, Archie could not spot anything that looked like it could possibly be used as a weapon.

A small voice in his head whispered, *except for the dinosaurs in the time portal.*

Archie ignored this tiny voice and drew himself up. He thought briefly of his Super Chickens. Summoning all of his courage, he stepped out from behind the trees and into the clearing.

"Hey!" he shouted. "Step away from the machine!"

At the sound of his voice Mr Franksman jumped. He whirled around and faced Archie, his eyes wild, his face dark and terrible.

"What? Who the..?" spluttered the groundskeeper. He gaped at Archie.

To Archie's dismay, Mr Franksman quickly composed himself. He took in the small figure of Archie standing all alone in his eagle mask and from

153

the visible calming of his demeanor it was clear he did not see him as a serious threat. The thin mouth drew itself into a faint smile.

"Oh. Just a pesky kid," he sneered. "Nothing to worry about. The plan will go ahead!"

"You need to stop this! It's crazy!" Archie shouted. "I… I won't let you do it!"

Mr Franksman gave a snort of laughter and turned to the oven-time-machine. He punched at a panel on its dented top and suddenly the front flashed bright with a brilliant glow of green, a flurry of numbers and letters appearing on a small screen.

"Seriously… you can't do this! You're going to hurt people. And… and…." stammered Archie.

"And what, boy? What? Those people out there? They'll get out of my way if they know what's good for them. And after tonight? No more fun fetes for the likes of you!" The groundskeeper gave another scornful laugh and turned his attention back to the oven-time-machine, waving his hand dismissively.

Archie felt his stomach clench. His fists balled up with angry tension. He felt desperate, hopeless

154

even, as he watched the man in navy blue turn away from him as though he was no more than a pesky ant.

He took a deep breath and blew it out softly through his mouth. He felt helpless but he knew he had to try, he had to do SOMETHING. He glanced behind him into the thicket of trees beyond. Trying to calm the tremble in his voice he spoke to the man again.

"I said, I won't let you do it. I'll stop you."

Not even bothering to turn and face him, the man replied, "Go home kid. You're on your own and there's nothing you can do to stop me. Whoever you are, it's better you just get out of here before it's too late."

Archie glanced behind him once more.

"I'm not on my own. And like I said, I WON'T let you do it."

He pursed his lips and whistled, then clucked his tongue twice. "Okay girls! It's time to teach this big bully a lesson. Let's go!"

From within the depths of the tree lined darkness behind him there came… absolutely nothing.

He groaned inside and tried again. "GIRLS! Come ON!"

Archie clucked his tongue three times more and spoke in a voice barely above a whisper. "Look. I KNOW you can do this. I'll… I'll double your feed tomorrow if you help me out here. PLEASE girls, come ON!"

For the briefest of moments, there was nothing more than the sound of a faint breeze swishing through the branches and the muted mutterings of the navy blue-clad man tinkering with his oven-machine.

And then, so slowly that it felt like time was standing still, here they came.

His girls. His CHICKENS.

Walking slowly but deliberately towards him and the crazy man.

With beady eyes and stiff wings held slightly aloft, the chickens moved forward to stand on either side of the small boy in his feathered mask.

Archie grinned and faced the groundskeeper once more.

"I told you. I'm not alone. And now, my Super Chickens are here and together we will stop your evil plan!"

Chapter Eighteen: Fight

For a moment Mr Franksman just stood staring blankly at the little group with a look of complete and utter disbelief on his face. Then his still face fractured with a burst of maniacal laughter.

"Chickens?" he spluttered. "You've... you've brought CHICKENS?"

Archie found this response rather irritating. His confidence had already taken a dive when his chickens failed to immediately respond to his calls. When they had finally appeared their superhero entrance had been less than convincing. His four largest hens - Lola, Coco, Rosie and Olive - had attempted a kind of slow motion hero swagger, fanning out in formation beside Archie as a show of team strength.

Unfortunately the combination of the forest darkness and their giant pom poms prevented Milk and Sugar from seeing clearly where they were going. When the other chickens stopped, they did not. Both of the silkies kept on walking, oblivious to what was in front of them. Milk ran straight into the back of Archie's legs. Sugar jumped in the air in surprise as she suddenly collided with the large, fluffy barrier that was Rosie's bottom. Rosie had growled angrily. Cringing, Archie had had to set Milk back onto her feet and break up the scuffle instigated by Rosie.

As the man in navy blue doubled over and shook with laughter, Archie mumbled a retort under his breath along the lines of "they're not just any chickens" and "teach you to laugh at us".

Mr Franksman continued to guffaw wildly, his face flushed and contorted. After considerable effort he managed to compose himself. He straightened up and wiped the tears streaming from his eyes.

"Chickens! What a surprise," he sniggered. "Well boy, if you insist on sticking around, I have no doubt they'll make a fine snack for my prehistoric visitors. They're due to arrive very shortly."

Mr Franksman threw Archie an evil grin.

"Let's invite them to join us now, shall we?"

And with that Mr Franksman reached out towards the front panel of the oven-time-machine and jabbed his finger on the large, red button.

"No!" Archie yelled as the machine whirred into life. The groundskeeper watched in delight, his elated face lit up by the glowing, swirling portal that had begun to take shape. As the portal grew larger and more clearly defined Mr Franksman retreated backwards, continuing to watch from a safe distance at the edge of the clearing.

Panic rising, Archie fumbled frantically within his backpack, trying to remember the plan he and Josh had sketched out. He pulled out a pair of headphones, jamming them down roughly over his ears. Quickly he extracted a dolphin torch and set it up on the ground facing the groundskeeper.

From a side pocket of the bag he withdrew a packet of grated cheese. He dug his hand into the packet and pulled out a fistful of pale yellow cheese strands.

"Girls! Get him!" cried Archie, flicking the torch on and flinging the cheese in the direction of the groundskeeper. "Hold him off while I disable the machine!"

He felt a savage burn of pleasure as the torch flared brightly and the cheese sailed through the air as if in slow motion. Blinded by the light, Mr Franksman threw up a hand to shield his eyes and stumbled backwards several steps. Before the first piece of cheese could touch the ground his chickens were in motion, wings flapping and legs pumping. At least, most of his chickens were in motion. Still unable to clearly see any of the action, the Smalls stood motionless beside Archie, their pom poms quivering as they tried to figure out what was going on.

"Rosie - GROW! Coco - SPEED!" yelled Archie. "And Smalls - go back to the trees and take cover!" He darted forward towards the time machine with a pair of wire cutters and a screwdriver grasped firmly in one hand.

Mr Franksman continued to back away as the chickens approached, their dark silhouettes backlit against the bright beam of light. Still holding one hand in front of his face to block the glare of the torch, he scrambled at his toolbelt with his free hand. Cursing, he pulled out a pencil and threw it at the oncoming feathered shapes.

Coco, who was rushing towards the cheese with incredible speed, easily swerved out of the path of the thrown pencil and darted out of sight amongst the trees. Like a tiny red spear the pencil landed point first in the ground directly in front of Olive, who had been following fast on Coco's heels. Olive gave a shrill whistle in fright. She lurched sideways and collided with Rosie, who growled and puffed out her feathers. Already Rosie was nearly twice the size of the other chickens, her footsteps thumping loudly as she stomped towards the scattered cheese. She and Olive arrived at the cheese bonanza at the same time. Pecking wildly at the yellow strands littering the ground, they scuffled and shoved each other out of the way, the groundskeeper forgotten in their frantic search. As Rosie and Olive scrabbled amongst themselves Olive's whistling became louder and Rosie grew still larger. Soon she towered over Olive, her fluffy bulk so

162

enormous that it blocked out the blinding light of the dolphin torch.

Mr Franksman lowered his hand from his face. His wild eyes fell upon the huge, hulking chicken and then moved past Rosie to spot the small form of Archie, who was pressing buttons and desperately snipping wires attached to the oven-time-machine.

The groundskeeper roared with rage.

"Oi!" he bellowed. "Get away from that machine!"

He yanked a small object from a clip on his belt and hurled it at Archie. The small object - which turned out to be a sunglasses case - turned end over end in the air. Just as it looked certain to hit Archie smack on the head there was a sharp metallic sound like the unsheathing of a sword and a gleaming brown figure leapt into the air. Another metallic clang rang out as the case hit the wing-shield of Lola and deflected away. It spun again through the air and bonked Olive right on the top of her head. For a moment Olive's eyes boggled crazily and the comb on her head jiggled. Then as her eyes regained focus, she stilled her head, opened her beak wide and began to whistle.

The high pitched whistle pierced the air, shrill and unrelenting. Mr Franksman gave a cry of pain and clutched his ears. A small, square, yellow object hurtled through the air. The groundskeeper had pulled a tape measure from his toolbelt and thrown it at Archie, just managing to release it before his hands flew to his ears. It arced high into the air and began to fall. The gleaming brown figure of Lola darted in once more, her wing-shield unsheathed and ready.

There was a second loud clang as the tape measure hit the sleek, curved surface of Lola's wing-shield. It rebounded off into the side of Archie's backpack, causing the bag to spew its contents everywhere. Cheese strands scattered all over the oven-time-machine. They were strewn across the surface of the machine's control panel and through its wiring, with some even vanishing into the depths of the swirling portal.

It was total chaos. Lights flashed and swirled in the near darkness. The shrill, ear-piercing whistling from Olive seemed to vibrate in the air. Mr Franksman continued to yell and moan, his hands pressed to his ears but unable to block out the sound.

Nearby, Rosie paused in her search for any last remaining cheese. Seemingly unbothered by the bursts of light or the deafening noise, she raised her enlarged head above her enormous body and gazed around. Her eyes narrowed as she spied the new trove of spilled cheese on the oven-time-machine. Leaves on the ground trembled and shook as Rosie stomped greedily towards Archie and the machine. There was a great flurry of air as Rosie flapped her wings twice and jumped. With a heavy thud she landed on the top of the machine, the metal screeching as her claws scrabbled for footing.

Archie, who had been trying desperately to remove the entire front panel with a screwdriver, hurriedly yanked his hands out of Rosie's way. Sparks flew and lights flashed as her huge talon-like claws gouged into the metal and several wires disconnected as her sharp beak pecked mercilessly at the scattered cheese.

All of the sudden the brightly lit panel on the front of the machine grew dark. The swirling portal expanded, growing larger and impossibly bright and forcing Archie to look away, before suddenly vanishing with a loud crack. Startled, both Archie and Rosie turned towards the unexpected noise. Rosie's hefty bottom swung around and clipped Archie, her expansive puffy behind knocking him sideways onto the ground. As he fell Archie felt something hard collide with his head. Stars swam before his eyes as he lay dazed on the ground. Shadowy figures seemed to pass in and out of his field of vision. He thought he glimpsed the man in navy blue hunched over the time machine once more, but couldn't be sure he wasn't imagining it. Archie blinked and tried to focus as the navy blue man seemed to vanish. He heard a sinister laugh that drifted away as swiftly as the man had, before everything faded to darkness and he lay still.

Chapter Nineteen: Flight

A soft but insistent beeping noise brought Archie back to his senses. He found himself still lying on the ground close to the machine. Though the front panel remained dark and the lights were no longer flashing, it seemed that the beeping noises were originating from somewhere inside the machine.

Peering down curiously at his face were three small faces, each fixed with a red comb and a pair of beady eyes set above pointy beaks. Lola, Olive and Rosie were standing around and observing him with interest. They had resumed their normal chicken form - Lola's wing-shield sheathed, Olive's beak closed and silent and Rosie back to simply puffy rather than gigantic.

He raised himself up on his elbows, wincing as he did so. His head felt tender but otherwise he did not appear to be hurt in any way. He looked around the little clearing. What had happened? Had Mr Franksman fled? Where were the rest of the chickens?

As Archie struggled to make sense of his situation, the beeping noise continued to demand his attention. He scrambled over to the oven-machine. It was badly dented, with claw marks pocked across its surface from Rosie's giant talons. He tugged at the front, roughly forcing it open. Inside the machine there was another panel, red numbers splashed on its face. It was not as brightly lit as the front panel had been, but instead looked more like a digital clock. Or a timer. With numbers counting down.

Squinting hard, he could just make out some small words printed underneath the red numbers.

SELF DESTRUCT SEQUENCE.

Horror flooded through Archie.

It was a countdown. The machine was going to explode.

Having foiled Mr Franksman's original plan, it appeared that the groundskeeper had set the machine to self-destruct in order to destroy any evidence and eliminate Archie in the process.

Archie knew he had to get out of there. He and his chickens had to get as far away from the machine as possible before the countdown got to zero.

He hauled himself to his feet and stood swaying unsteadily, one hand gripping the oven-machine.

Rosie, Lola and Olive were still grouped beside him, studying him intently.

"Girls! You need to get out of here," cried Archie, shooing them with his hands. "Quickly! Get back to the hen-icopter." He hustled the chickens along, struggling to keep his balance, before he pitched forward onto his knees.

The three chickens looked alarmed and jumped back several paces. Then Lola gave a little flick of her head to the others, signalling them to follow her as she trotted away into the trees.

Archie watched them go, feeling a mixture of relief and despair. He clambered to his feet and slowly stumbled after them. His head reeled. He felt dizzy and sick but he had to move, even though he knew it was probably not fast enough. Every few steps his giddy head became too much and he was forced to pause, bending over with his hands on his knees.

Suddenly he felt the air swirl around him. A flurry of leaves danced on the ground and Archie felt his body propelled forward of its own accord. Like a rag doll controlled by a small child he found himself racing forward with his arms flapping and legs turning over.

Coco had dashed out of nowhere, zipping in and under Archie and forcing him into motion. Her speed kept his legs moving automatically, propelling him ahead. The pair of them sped through the trees.

Up ahead Archie could see moving shapes. Two small, white blobs that seemed to gleam in the darkness. The Smalls! Archie's heart leapt with joy at the sight of them. Looking past the two silkies he spied another moving shape, this one darker and taller and travelling swiftly. Mr Franksman. The groundskeeper was running unhindered through the forest, looking very much like he was going to make a clean getaway.

Archie gritted his teeth. He couldn't bear the thought of Mr Franksman getting away scot-free. Not after the horrible acts he had attempted. He shook his head to clear the last of the dizziness away and began to pump his arms and legs with renewed energy.

"Speed Coco, SPEED!" he cried. "Stop him!"

The small brown chicken narrowed her eyes and zoomed forward. Archie lurched as she left him behind, forcing him to control his body without Coco propelling him along. Her legs were a blur as she hurtled past shrubs and trees, rapidly closing the distance between Archie and the fleeing man in navy blue.

Coco zoomed past the Smalls and vanished from sight, dust and leaves billowing in her wake. Then the two white chickens were lifted off their feet. The force of Coco's slipstream picked them up and took their legs out from under them. Milk and Sugar collided headfirst in midair, their fluffy pom-poms squashed flat as their heads made contact with each other. They bounced apart and tumbled onto the ground.

Archie gasped in amazement. As the Smalls pitched over, the two silkie chickens suddenly began multiplying. Small white shapes erupted from their pom poms like puffy popcorn. Two became four, then eight, then sixteen. More and more round white chickens burst forth until Archie could no longer count them all. They tumbled and rolled and bounced on the ground like golf balls.

As he drew closer Archie could see that they were not the soft and delightfully fluffy chickens he was familiar with. Their feathers stood out like rigid spikes, their bodies solid and unforgiving. Like a flood of spiky marbles the replicated Smalls streamed towards Mr Franksman. The vast white wave came tossing and tumbling, until it reached the groundskeeper and swept his feet out from beneath him. For a few seconds he was carried along by the wave, his boot clad feet bobbing comically in the air.

There was a flash of brown as Coco streaked in, drawing a line through the white wave as clearly as a marker pen. Replica Smalls bounced up into the air on either side of her line like the wake of a speedboat. She rocketed past Mr Franksman in a blur of brown feathers, causing the groundskeeper to do a clumsy backflip in the air. He hit the ground with a heavy thud.

Archie whooped.

The swell of replicated Smalls frothed and seemed to fizzle out, like a wave breaking on the seashore. As Archie watched the carpet of puffy white marbles bumped and squeezed itself, the number of small white shapes quickly shrinking as they began to recombine. Finally, only the original two Smalls stood before him.

He crouched down to scoop up Milk and Sugar, giving them a joyous squeeze.

"Omigod! What was THAT? You two were AMAZING!" he squealed.

He pressed his face to their feathers which were deliciously soft and fluffy.

But before Archie could say any more words of praise he heard the faint sound of the countdown timer in the distance. The beeping had increased in volume and tempo, a brief staccato beat that rang out loudly before it came to an abrupt end.

There was a silent pause, then a sudden flash of white light as the night was torn apart.

Still crouched and clutching the Smalls, Archie felt the hot blast of the explosion hurtling towards him. He braced himself for the impact but it never came.

Lola had come to their rescue. She was pressed close against Archie and the two silkies, with her glinting wings curved in a steely dome that shielded them from the explosive blast. Hot air whooshed past, sending leaves and flying branches whirling through the air. Archie heard clanging and scratching as airborne debris hit Lola's wing-shield and deflected away. Through squinted eyes he thought he glimpsed Mr Franksman lying on the ground a short distance away, his navy work clothes covered in dust. He wasn't moving, but Archie did not get the opportunity to inspect him more closely. The swirling dust choked the air and forced him to squeeze his eyes tightly shut.

Gradually the force of the explosion subsided and the air around Archie settled. The dust in the air began to clear, leaving behind a thin, grainy film on the surface of everything around him. Archie blinked hard and wiped his face with the inside of his shirt to clear some of the grit from his eyes.

Lowering the Smalls to the ground he stood up and looked around. Mr Franksman was nowhere to be seen. The groundskeeper must have made his escape in the midst of the blast, before the dust settled.

Archie felt a guilty pang of relief. He had not wanted anybody to get seriously hurt, even the evil groundskeeper. He just hoped that Mr Franksman had learned his lesson well enough from the encounter and would put aside any thoughts of future sinister plots and schemes.

"Alright girls. Let's go find the others," said Archie.

He and his little cluster of chickens turned and began to pick their way through the debris-strewn forest. They had not gone far when Archie nudged aside a branch on the ground to clear the way for the chickens. As he shoved at it with his foot he noticed a small, metallic-looking panel lying underneath. He stooped to pick it up, turning the object over in his hands. It looked to be a control panel of sorts.

With a sudden jolt he realised that this must be a part from the now destroyed oven-time-machine.

Archie's fingers ran gingerly over the dusty electrical components on the circuit board, tracing them along a series of plastic-coated wires, their frayed ends evidence of being violently severed from their host. His mind swam with possibilities as he continued to make his way back to the edge of the forest.

Gradually the darkness of the forest grew lighter until finally they emerged from the trees by the fenceline and into the still, clear night.

Archie took a deep breath, filling his lungs with crisp, cool air. He blew out a huge sigh of relief. Perched neatly on the fence were Rosie, Olive and Coco, looking relaxed and unharmed.

As he walked over to join the other half of his flock the air was suddenly split by another explosive bang.

Immediately Archie cowered. His hands instinctively flew up to shield himself from the blast he expected to follow but even as he did so he realized that this explosion was different.

A second crackle rang through the air. There was no blast of hot air, no flurry of flying branches.

Archie lowered his hands and raised his head. A bright burst of colour lit up the night sky as more crackles and bangs rang out.

Fireworks! The Fete fireworks had begun!

The heavens flashed with colour - white, gold, purple, red and green - as the spectacular pyrotechnic show danced above them.

His six chickens gathered around him and together they stood, faces raised to the sky.

Nobody said a word.

No words were needed.

The little group remained silent and still, basking in the aftermath of their achievements.

They had done it.

Against the odds, the Incredible Rooster and the Super Chickens had thwarted the evil groundskeeper and his wicked plan.

Chapter Twenty: Code Names

As the sun rose on a brand new day and bathed the yard in soft early morning light, the chickens filed sleepily out of their coop. They were certainly tired from the events of the night gone by but it was not in the nature of a chicken to sleep in. Instead, they went about their business the same as usual, though perhaps with a slightly higher degree of clumsiness.

Rosie huffed and sat down in the middle of the yard, scraping her beak angrily into the grass as though it was the cause of her fatigue. Olive shuffled over to the automatic chicken feeder, which was similar to a foot pedal rubbish bin but shaped low and long to accommodate two or three chickens side-by-side. Olive stomped her foot on the lever of the automatic feeder but when the lid snapped open she simply stood, staring into space, apparently having forgotten why she was there in the first place. She removed her foot and the lid clanged shut, only to then replace her foot on the lever and repeat it all over again.

Eventually Lola decided that a chicken meeting was warranted and called all of the hens together. Rosie had outright refused to budge, remaining stubbornly rooted on the grass like a giant puffy toadstool. Rolling her eyes, Lola decided it was probably best not to argue and so she gathered the others around Rosie instead.

"Alright girls," she began. "That was certainly an adventure last night! I think we should all be very proud of ourselves. And of our brave Chicken-Boy too."

All of the others, except for Rosie, gave a low murmur of agreement.

"So," Lola continued, "I think we should do something to acknowledge our achievements. To recognize that we, as chickens, are SPECIAL."

Nobody said anything for a few moments. Rosie had now tucked her head under her wing and appeared to be dozing.

Then Olive's face lit up.

"Special… Special food!" she said excitedly. "We should have special food. Lots of it! Like the special food Chicken-Boy brings us from the giant coop beyond the gate. Yes. I think that would be wonderful." She gazed dreamily at the gate as if expecting it to swing open at that very moment and for a mountain of special food to magically float towards them.

Lola gave a little cough. "Uh... no. That's not quite what I had in mind."

Seeing the look on Olive's face morphing from dreamy to disgruntled, she quickly added, "...but I'm certain Chicken-Boy won't forget about how we helped him and will bring us some special food when he wakes up."

"I was thinking," she continued, "that we should have special NAMES. Super chicken titles to match our special talents."

Lola turned her gaze to Coco. "You should be FLASH COCO."

Next, she faced Olive. "And you, Olive, should be BLACK WHISTLE."

Lola stretched out her neck and pecked the back of the giant puffy toadstool. It twitched and rose to its feet, as Rosie finally opened her eyes and rejoined the conversation.

"Welcome back, Rosie!" said Lola drily. "I think your special name should be ROSEN-HULK."

Rosie made a low noise somewhere between a grunt and a growl.

Last of all, Lola located the two silkies, Milk and Sugar. She looked down at the pair of them.

"Smalls. What a surprise package you turned out to be," she said. "There's nothing else for it. It fits. You will be THE SMALLS."

The Smalls remained motionless, their pom pom heads turned towards Lola. She gave a small shrug. "As they say, if the shoe fits..."

"But chickens don't wear shoes!" scoffed Olive.

"It's just a -" Lola began.

"And shoes would look simply AWFUL on a chicken!" said Rosie.

"Shoes? Who said what now about shoes?" blurted Coco. "Do we have to wear shoes now? I've never worn shoes before and although I agree with Rosie that shoes would most certainly look awful on a chicken I would be happy to wear shoes if that's what you want us to do. And of course as long as Chicken-Boy is happy for us to wear shoes as well though I don't know if he will have thought about what wearing shoes will do for my speed."

"I don't care if you or Chicken-Boy want us to wear them. I absolutely REFUSE to wear shoes!" Rosie declared huffily.

Lola stared at the three of them. "If the shoe fits. It's an EXPRESSION. It's just a figure of speech." She mumbled something inaudible along the lines of "tiny brains".

"Just calm down and forget anything about shoes. We're talking about our special chicken names, ok?" said Lola.

Rosie gave Lola a mock salute with her wing. "Yes Captain! Whatever you say, Captain!"

Olive thought for a moment. "Captain. That has a nice ring to it," she said. "Yes. Captain Lola!"

Lola tilted her head and considered this. Then she drew herself up to her fullest height and puffed out her chest.

"Yes. That's perfect. Captain Lola!"

The little flock stood in the middle of the yard, allowing their new super chicken names to sink in.

It was at that precise moment that Archie pushed open the gate and wandered out into the backyard. He took in the sight of his super chickens gathered all together in the middle of the yard like a team huddle. He half expected them to stretch their wingtips to the middle and yell "Super chickens!" on the count of three. Instead the chickens merely turned their heads towards him.

Archie greeted his flock. "Good morning, you wonderful chickens! I have something for you."

From behind his back he drew out a bowl filled to the brim with all sorts of chicken treats. He placed the bowl on the ground in the middle of the chicken huddle and watched, smiling, as the chickens converged on it.

With his other hand he pulled out his notepad, flipping it open to the most recent page.

"I've got another surprise for you," he said, his grin widening. "Since you are all very special chickens, super chickens in fact, I've come up with some special code names for you."

He held up the notepad on which he had written:

Super Chicken Code Names

Lola - CAPTAIN LOLA

Olive - BLACK WHISTLE

Rosie - ROSEN-HULK

Coco - FLASH COCO

Milk and Sugar - THE SMALLS

Chapter Twenty-One: Aftermath

When Archie returned to school on Monday it was not without a certain degree of trepidation. He and his chickens had foiled the groundskeeper's plan, but he had no idea what Mr Franksman had done afterwards. What had happened to him? Had he recognized Archie even with his eagle mask disguise? After the fireworks had finished, Archie had briefly spoken to Josh over the walkie-talkies and filled him in on all that had happened, but neither of them had seen the groundskeeper since. Was he now skulking in his shed, already plotting an even more sinister scheme?

Archie slung his backpack onto the rack and knelt down to extract his water from the side pocket. As he opened the lid and took a swig from the bottle he heard a sudden rush of footsteps and then felt a warm hand press down heavily on his shoulder. He gave a tiny involuntary squeak, slopping cold water down the front of his shirt. His head whipped around, fully expecting to see a pair of black boots and navy work pants.

It was Josh, grinning broadly at him, his blonde hair mussed and sweaty from running across the playground.

"Smooth, Arch!" he teased.

"Omigod. Josh!" groaned Archie. "Don't freak me out like that!"

"Yeah yeah, I know. You thought I was Mr Franksman," said Josh, still grinning. "Don't worry, I'm almost CERTAIN he has no idea it was you. I just saw him. His hair's all like, singed on the ends and he was stomping around just as cranky as usual. But he didn't seem to be looking for anyone in particular, so I think your disguise worked! The secret identity of The Incredible Rooster remains intact!"

Archie closed the lid of his water bottle and tried to wipe the water from his shirt.

"Nope, I think we pulled off the plan PERFECTLY. You and the Super Chickens were AWESOME. No-one was hurt, the time machine was destroyed and nobody noticed the explosion because the fireworks started at pretty much the same time," continued Josh. "Plus you found that control board piece, which looks pretty interesting. Could be some kind of super advanced technology. We'll definitely have to investigate that at some point."

"Yeah, I guess you're right," conceded Archie. "Everything did work out pretty well in the end."

"ALMOST everything," said Josh, lowering his voice furtively. "If we do undertake another undercover mission, remind me to never, EVER eat another dagwood dog again! They were dodgy alright. That battered sausage lured me in with its delicious deep-fried batter and shiny red sauce, but it gave me nothing but regret. I spent half the night on the toilet. Pretty sure what came out of my butt was toxic enough to wipe out half the school! No portaloo in the world would be equipped to handle that amount of sh-"

"Eewww! That is seriously disgusting... and also WAY too much information!" Archie held up a hand to stop the verbal diarrhoea coming from Josh but he too was grinning. "I do remember asking you if it was really a good time to eat a dagwood dog."

"Yeah, I guess you did. My answer should have been never - it's never a good time to eat a dagwood dog!" laughed Josh. "Anyway, speaking of disgusting. There's a gigantic toad in the playground near the water play. Ryan spotted it and it's HUGE! Let's go check it out!"

Still laughing, the two boys sprinted off towards the playground. As they ran along the path Archie glanced at the solitary building on the other side of a low chain-link fence. Mr Franksman's shed. The roller door was open and the interior was lit up brightly. The man in navy blue was returning a leaf blower to its correct space amongst his wall of equipment.

Archie felt a familiar tingle of apprehension at the sight of the groundskeeper.

Except now, a small but defiant feeling of resolve rose within him. Mr Franksman might well be working on a new evil plan. There was no way of knowing.

But Archie knew that he was not alone. He knew that no matter what was to come, he would face it head on.

He would be ready, together with his accidental chicken heroes.

CAPTAIN LOLA

ROSEN-HULK

BLACK WHISTLE

FLASH COCO

THE SMALLS

Well done and thanks for making it this far!

A huge thank you for checking out my book. As a small independent publisher, it means a lot and I hope I have made a difference in your reading journey. If you have a minute, sharing your honest feedback would be amazing - it really helps others find the book and I love hearing your thoughts – I see and read every review!

To leave your feedback on Amazon:

1. Open your camera app
2. Point your mobile device at the below QR code
3. The review page will appear in your web browser

OR visit amazon.com.au/dp/0975613227#customerReviews

OR find this book in Your Orders on the Amazon app

Thank you from Clucky Feathers Books!

amazon amazon.com/author/anitasachlikidis

instagram.com/cluckyfeathersbooks

More hilarious Accidental Chicken Heroes adventures

Made in the USA
Monee, IL
10 November 2024

69755507R00118